FLIRTING WITH MY BROTHER'S BILLIONAIRE BEST FRIEND

A BLUE MOUNTAIN SWEET ROMANTIC COMEDY

CINDY RAY HALE

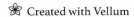

For my daughter Lillie. You brighten my day with your smiles. I'm so glad you're in my family.

1

JENNI

The wind whips through my hair as I gallop down the trail atop my horse, Marshmallow. I love this feeling, the powerful movements of the horse beneath me, the thrill that goes through my body as we reach top speeds. The tiniest of leaves are beginning to appear on the trees around me, and there are pink and white flowers appearing throughout the forest.

As I near the lake on my parents' property, my older brother Ronnie and his lifelong best friend, Langston Keith, come into view as I round the corner and the foliage opens to reveal the water. A loud splash sounds as Langston shoves Ronnie into the water. We spent our youth at this lake, and after all these years, I've never seen them swimming when it was this cold.

The Keith and Finley kids were tutored and traveled the world together as our parents took us on our many vacations. Our families have been friends for generations, and we both live in the small town of Blue Mountain, Georgia. Langston was always teasing me, pulling pranks like dropping a frog into my bunk when we were traveling together on his family's yacht. I wasn't afraid to get him back either though. I filled a bucket full of hermit crabs and dumped them on him when he was asleep at night.

Our relationship has been like that for as long as I can remember. We're always joking around with lots of shenanigans back and forth. One would think that we would have grown out of it by now, but we really haven't.

They're both in their thirties, but they're acting like they're teens. It's something I love about both of them. They can sit around a boardroom table and discuss the health of a worldwide corporation one moment, but they still know how to let out their inner kid.

I slow Marshmallow as we approach the dock.

"What are you guys doing? You do realize it's April, right?" I call to them.

Langston spreads his arms wide. He has on jeans, and his torso is bare, revealing his chiseled abs. "Just getting in some exercise."

Ronnie climbs up the ladder on the dock and shakes the water off him like one of the golden retrievers my parents breed. The frigid lake water lands on us, and Marshmallow takes a step back.

Smart horse. I wouldn't want to be near these two either with their antics. Okay, that may not be entirely true since I did lead Marshmallow right to them.

"You still haven't told me why you're swimming when it's forty-seven degrees out," I drawl as I swing down from Marshmallow's back.

"Ronnie dared me to a swim," Langston tells me.

"And you haven't even gotten in the water," Ronnie shoots back at him.

"What are you up to, Jenni?" Langston smiles at me, dimples and all. I've always loved Langston's dimples. They're very... him.

I stroke Marshmallow's mane. "The vet cleared Valentine for racing again. So get ready for your Thunder to eat Valentine's dust."

"What about Kingpen?" Langston asks. "Are you still racing him?"

"I've decided to retire him." I keep my eyes focused on his face. It's not like I haven't seen Langston shirtless before, but I don't want to gawk either. The guy is built, and it can be... distracting.

"You sure you want to risk racing Valentine after his injury?" Langston asks.

"I'm trusting what the vet says on this one."

Langston frowns.

"What's that look for?" I walk toward Langston. "You scared Valentine is going to take Thunder down?"

Valentine has beaten Thunder race after race, but since his injury three months ago, Thunder has been beating Kingpen, which is why I decided to retire the older horse. After Valentine's injury, I was worried he'd never see the track again, but the amazing horse has healed well, surprising us all.

Langston scoffs. "I'm hardly scared. You should know me well enough by now to know that."

I smirk at him. "Mmm. I know you well enough to know that under all this macho stuff is a little boy who's scared of being taken down by a girl."

"You look a little overdressed," Langston says.

I give him a once over. "I'm pretty sure you have that backwards."

"You mean I'm underdressed." He grins.

I wave a hand dismissively. "You know what I mean. You're crazy, and I'm the one dressed properly."

"You'll change your mind about that in a minute." He wraps his arms around my waist and lifts me over his shoulder.

I shriek, "Langston Anderson Keith, you put me down right this minute." I pound on his back, but he only laughs, a rumble beneath my fists. His back is so hard that it hurts to punch into the muscle there.

The next thing I know, I'm being tossed into cold water that feels like a thousand icy needles pricking my skin. Thankfully, it's not too deep, and I'm able to push off the bottom to emerge in time to take a breath. With all these clothes on, I'd sink to the bottom if it were over my head. Water splashes into my face as Langston lands in the water next to me.

I push away the wet hair plastered to my face. Ronnie is out of the water and back up on the dock, belly laughing. Then he grabs Marshmallow's reins and ties him to a fence post. It's a good thing, because it's not like I had a chance to do it.

Langston pops up next to me with a wide grin that lights up his entire face. His eyes are sparkling, and I can't help but feel some of the joy exuding from him.

"I should have seen that coming," I say. It's not the first time he's tossed me into a lake. To be fair, I've done my fair share of pushing him into various bodies of water when he's least suspecting it.

Ronnie jumps in with us, and Langston stretches out in the water, taking long strokes away from where Ronnie's splashing in the water. I trudge through the lake next to them and then follow where Langston is going. I don't even care that my clothes are heavy and wet or that it's going to be even more freezing when I finally climb out of here and the wind hits me.

Langston turns to me with that same grin. "Enjoying the water?"

I return his smile. There's no way I'm giving him the satisfaction of knowing how miserable I feel. "Oh, yes. That is just what I had in mind for my morning ride. The water's refreshing."

He's no dummy, though. The guy can see right through me. After twenty years of teasing, it's no surprise.

"It's a good thing the guest house has a dryer," he says.

"And a shower," Ronnie says, swimming up to us.

"And a coffeemaker," Langston says.

"Doesn't Mom have people coming to stay in it later today?" I ask Ronnie.

"We'll make sure it gets cleaned up after we're done," Ronnie says.

"Or you two can just walk back in your birthday suits while I use the shower." Why did I say that? I conjure images of fluffy bunnies and kittens so I don't think of Langston naked.

"We brought four-wheelers," Langston says. "We drove them over from my place."

I glance over to see them parked behind some bushes. I hadn't even noticed them there before.

Langston's extensive acreage borders my parents' property. I have a place of my own in town, but I come over to spend a lot of time at my parents' because I keep Marshmallow and Valentine stabled there.

There's a rope swing off to the side, and Langston and Ronnie swim over to it.

"What are you guys doing now?" I ask.

6

"Proving that it's not too cold to swim," Langston calls to me from over his shoulder.

"I think you've already proved that," I say.

"Well, this just extra proves it," Langston yells back.

"If that makes you feel tougher somehow." I roll my eyes. But the truth is, I like this about Langston. He's carefree and fun, always full of life. He likes to run his mouth too. His family, especially his youngest brother, Kaison, call him out on it all the time.

Langston climbs out of the lake, his muscles flexing as he moves, and Ronnie follows.

"I think I'll just stay in here for a bit." I could run over to the lake house and shower off, but then that would show weakness. And I can't allow that, now can I? Anyway, I'm starting to get used to the water. Either that or my body is losing all feeling.

Langston grabs the rope swing and launches himself into the air, just like when we were kids.

He hoots and hollers as he sails over the water, landing with a splash that reaches all the way to where I'm standing in the water, thirty feet away.

His head emerges, and he roars, beating on his chest like a barbarian landing his first kill.

"I don't know how I feel about all this testosterone." But I'm used to it from being around Ronnie and Langston, and Langston's four brothers so much.

Family is everything to me. Ronnie is two years older than me, and I was a tomboy, always tagging along with the boys. Langston is the second of the Keith boys and is a couple of years older than me, the same age as Ronnie. I grew up playing with Ashton, who is my age. He lives in Singapore now, so I only see him for holidays and the odd visit back.

My mom likes to sit around with Langston's mom, Laurie, talking about how much they want grandbabies. Langston's mom has a granddaughter, two-year-old Angel, who is Callie's little girl from her first marriage, and Callie is now married to Langston's older brother, Weston. But my mom doesn't have any grandkids, since Ronnie and I haven't made any headway in the relationship department. It's something that makes me sad. I've always wanted to be a mom, despite the fact that I grew up a tomboy and hated dolls. And nieces and nephews wouldn't be so bad either.

Langston swims up to me. "You look like you're a million miles away."

I turn to look at him. "Nope. I'm right here. And I'm ready for some coffee and a hot shower."

"Me too."

"Good thing the guest house has three showers." Ronnie swims up to us.

"Yeah, because otherwise, you'd be sitting in wet clothes until one of us got out of the shower," Langston says.

"You're assuming I would have let you go in first," Ronnie teases.

It's ridiculous because I know Ronnie would never be the type to make Langston sit in wet clothes while he enjoyed a nice, warm shower.

I get out of the water, and the wind hits me. I grit my teeth against the chill.

"Hey," Langston says, coming next to me. "At least it's not below freezing. Forty-seven isn't that bad."

"Yeah, just a nice spring day," I bite out, teeth chattering.

He pulls a dry jacket out of his backpack and puts it around my shoulders. I don't comment and accept the kind gesture. It makes up for the fact that he threw me in. But only a little.

After calling a groomsman to take Marshmallow back to the stable, we cross the lawn to the guest house, Langston and Ronnie on either side of me. Langston is close enough that I can see the goose-bumps rising on his skin. The guy must be freezing.

Ronnie is wrapped up in his towel. I key in the garage code, and we file into the house.

We're greeted by Rosie, one of the staff members, who is mopping the rustic stone floors. She's thin, early twenties, and wearing earbuds as she works. She pulls them out.

"I'm so sorry, Rosie," I say. "Can we use the showers? Someone thought it was a good idea to take a swim in April." I shoot Langston a scathing look.

"You must be freezing!" Rosie says. She's employed by my parents, but she cleans for me as well. I also have a cook and a guy to manage the grounds. Nothing like the extensive staff my parents keep to manage their twenty-thousand-square-foot home, and they often have guests visiting, like my mom's family from India.

"Sorry to mess up the bathrooms and to disturb you while you're cleaning," I say.

"Oh, it's no problem at all. Go get warm. It won't take me long to wipe them down again." She waves us away.

"Thank you, Rosie," Ronnie calls as we split up to go to our separate showers.

I sprint up the cedar staircase and head to the master bath since Ronnie and Langston went for the bathroom on the main floor and the one in the basement. I strip off the wet clothes, leaving them in a pile on the floor, making a mental note to tell Mom about how sweet Rosie is about us messing up the place right before guests are due.

I step into the stream of steaming hot water and sigh. It's such a relief to finally get warm again. I scrub the pond scum out of my hair with the random bottle of shampoo someone left in the shower. Thankfully, there's conditioner too, or I'd never get the tangles out of my overabundance of hair.

There's a knock, and Rosie calls to me through the cracked door. "Do you want me to put your wet things in the dryer for you?"

"Yes, please."

Her voice gets louder as she steps into the room and bends down to pick them up. "Langston mentioned that you don't have dry clothes with you. I can have some of your clothes sent over while you're showering, since these will take a while to dry."

"Thank you. That would be wonderful."

"In the meantime, there's a robe hooked onto the bathroom door you can use," Rosie says before leaving.

I finish my shower and dry off before I wrap up in the robe.

I go downstairs, and Ronnie and Langston are sitting around in pink fluffy bathrobes, watching something on Netflix.

"Oh, I like the new look, guys."

"Do you think it enhances my complexion?" Langston frames his face with his hands.

"It really brings out the color in your cheeks." I take a seat on the couch next to him. "Where did you find the pink bathrobes? All I got was this boring white one."

"They were hanging up."

"Mine came with shoes too." Langston models his feet in pink fuzzy flip-flops.

"I think those are my mom's," Ronnie says.

"Didn't you guys bring extra clothes?" I change the subject.

"We weren't really planning to swim, so no," Ronnie says. "We're just waiting for our stuff to dry."

"Rosie's having someone bring me clothes from home."

"That's what I should have done," Ronnie says.

"You really think Valentine will be ready to race again?" Langston must really be shaking in his boots if he's bringing it up again.

"Do you feel threatened?" I ask with a challenge in my voice and a smile I can't help.

He scoffs. "Hardly. I'm pretty secure in Thunder's ability to dominate the race."

"I guess we'll have to see about that," I say. "Valentine might just prove you wrong."

2

LANGSTON

"*L*angston, you're home," my mom says when I come in the door. She's sitting on the couch with some sort of container of food on the coffee table near her.

"Hey, Mom. How did you get in here?" It's pretty typical for her to randomly show up in my house, so I should know better by now than to even bother asking.

"Stella let me in."

She's referring to my housekeeper, who is close to the family. Stella was my sister-in-law's maid of honor at her wedding to my brother.

"I brought you some of my home-baked muffins." She stands and hands me the container.

"That was nice of you. But you didn't have to do that. You know I have Powell to cook for me," I say, referring to the world-class chef I employ.

"I know. But I was in the mood to bake." The truth is, she doesn't have to bake either. She has her cook, Lidia, to create tasty treats for her.

I wander into the kitchen, and she follows me there. It's dark, and I speak to the device controlling my home to get the lights to turn on. When the room is well-lit, I put the muffins on the counter and open the lid.

"I'll never get used to the crazy technology you have in your house," Mom complains.

"It's called a smart home." I worked with an architect to design my house myself when I was twenty. I've had it frequently updated over the years with all the latest innovations. My mom hates it because she can't figure out how to get any of it to work.

"I know. You've told me plenty of times."

I can't help smiling. It's a conversation we've had a lot. Mom loves social media, but her house is far from technologically advanced.

I pull out a blueberry lemon muffin and peel off the wrapper. I sit at my table so I don't get crumbs all over the floor. Even though I have a team of people to keep my house clean, I don't like making messes. My older brother Weston tells me I shouldn't worry about it, that it creates job security for my workers. I guess he has a point, but I'm still a bit of a neat freak.

The sweet and tart flavors of the muffin dance

around on my tastebuds. "This muffin is good, Mom," I say after I've chewed and swallowed my first bite.

"I was thinking, dear..." Mom starts.

Here we go. The real reason she came over. Whenever Mom says she's been thinking, I get worried. It never turns out well.

"It's been two years since you broke up with Sarah. Isn't it about time you found that special someone?"

Sarah left me for someone else, and the last thing I want to do is face that kind of situation again. It's easier being single. "You already have Weston married off, and Kaison is well on his way. Isn't that good enough?" I shouldn't be surprised that Mom is hounding me about getting married. She did the same thing to my brothers.

"I hate seeing you all alone." She reaches out and puts a hand on my arm. "I know your breakup with Sarah was rough, but you deserve to be happy, too."

I cringe at her words. My breakup with Sarah really isn't my favorite topic. "I am happy," I grumble. I have to wonder if the baked goods are a bribe to get me to open up about my feelings.

"What about Jenni?" She scoots another muffin toward me, like that's going to get me to consider her suggestion even more.

"Jenni... What about her?" I play dumb. Mom and Dad have been trying to get Jenni to marry one of us boys for years. First, it was Weston, but he married his assistant, Callie, instead. Weston was never into Jenni, anyway.

Let's be clear. Jenni is gorgeous. She's funny and driven and super smart. But there's this problem. "Ronnie would kill me if I laid a finger on his sister."

"It's not up to him. Meera and I have been planning to get our kids married off to each other since you were babies. We couldn't marry Ronnie to any of our kids because we never had a daughter, but Jenni... She would make a wonderful wife and mother." My mom gets this wistful look in her eyes.

"Jenni is more than just a baby factory," I say, suddenly annoyed.

Mom's eyes light up like she's excited to see me defending her. "Yes, I know. She's a strong, capable woman, but she's also capable of giving me another grandbaby." Her eyes turn greedy, like she's desperate to fill her house with children.

"And so is Callie. Angel is two years old now. She can become a big sister."

Mom gets this huge smile on her face. "Oh, believe me, I've already talked to them. They're working on it."

I grimace. "Gross, Mom. I don't want to hear about that."

"Well, it's how you get babies. It's not gross. It's a gift from God."

"It's gross when it's my brother. I'd rather not hear about them working on anything."

"We're getting off track," Mom says. "So you're worried about Ronnie getting upset? I'll talk to him and explain the situation."

"What? You can't do that." I'd just end up driving her away like all the other women in my life, and I've enjoyed her friendship too much to lose it.

"Well, why not?"

"Jenni isn't livestock to be auctioned off." She's so much more than that.

Mom wrinkles her nose. "It sounds awful when you put it like that."

"Jenni and I are nothing more than friends. And that's the way it's going to stay." Anyway, I'm pretty sure she'd laugh in my face if I asked her out, and I'm not in the mood to be humiliated.

"Oh, Langston. Why do you have to be so stubborn?"

I jut my chin out and fold my arms. "I'm not stubborn. I'm smart. I know when certain things should be left alone."

Something that looks like fear crossed with frustration creeps into Mom's eyes.

I furrow my brow. "Don't make that face. It's not the end of the world if some of your kids don't get married."

"I just don't see why you couldn't have tried to work it out with your ex-wife," Mom pouts. "I could have a whole slew of grandbabies by now. My one kid to get married and then ends it before any babies could come into the picture."

"I tried everything I could to make that marriage work. I can't help it if Amanda wanted to leave." And then, years later, Sarah decided to leave too, adding more salt to the abandonment wound I've been nursing for almost a decade.

She takes a muffin for herself. "But you didn't go after her either."

"I knew it was useless. If Amanda wanted to leave, who was I to stop her?"

I've given up on finding a woman who wants me for me. Putting myself out there isn't worth the pain.

~

 he next day, I'm driving down Main Street to meet up with Weston and Dad at Harvey's, a mom and pop diner that sells the best burgers and shakes you'll find anywhere. We're planning to discuss some business. I pull into the parking lot and Weston's Mercedes is already there, next to Dad's Lamborghini.

In a town as small as Blue Mountain, the Keiths and Finleys stick out as the only two wealthy families in town. But we don't really keep to ourselves. We love to be involved with the community. The townspeople have been used to us being around for generations.

When I get inside, Dad and Weston already have a table. I slide into the booth next to Dad. "Have you guys ordered yet?"

Dad is still in his suit from work. It seems like he hardly wears anything else. Weston and I both take after him, with the same dark hair and eyes. While I keep a beard, the two of them are clean shaven.

"We were just about to." Dad rubs his clean-shaven jaw.

I come here enough to know what I want.

Dolores, an older woman with frizzy red hair comes up to us to take our order.

"I'll take the bacon cheeseburger with extra cheese, fries, and a chocolate shake." My mouth is watering just thinking about the enormous amount of calories I'm about to consume.

"I'll have the usual." Dad still has his menu untouched in front of him.

"And me too." Weston hands her his.

"I don't know why I bother giving you Keiths a menu anyway," Dolores teases, her neon pink lips curling up as she takes Dad's menu from him and rests it on one of her wide hips.

Dad chuckles. "We change it up sometimes," he insists.

I glance over to see that Dad and Weston already have drinks. "Can I get a Coke with my dinner as well?"

"Of course, sweetie." Dolores gives me a cheerful

smile. "Anything else before I put this order in, or are you guys set?"

"I think that'll do it," Dad says.

The conversation turns to official business stuff for Keith Enterprises, Dad's commercial real estate corporation. "There's a property that just became available in Singapore. I've had my eye on it for years. Ashton just called and told me about it."

Dolores brings me my Coke, and I take a sip as we continue our discussion. Weston and my dad do a lot of work in Atlanta, but we all work remotely too. I prefer to stay in Blue Mountain, which is why I built a house here. I like the quiet, small-town feel. Weston also has a house in town and splits his time between Blue Mountain and Atlanta fairly evenly. He has a penthouse in Atlanta as well.

I go to set down my glass, and I look up to see Jenni and Ronnie walking past just in time for her to collide with my hand, sloshing Coke all over me. It drips down the front of me and pools into my lap.

"Oh, I'm so sorry." She reaches across the table to the napkin holder and fights with it to get a wad of napkins out. She grunts as she pulls at it, and they finally come free, flying all over the table. "Great. I'm just making it worse."

"No," I joke. "It's already soaking up some of the mess."

She grabs a handful of napkins and dabs at my

dress shirt, moving my tie to get the spot beneath it that's soaking into my chest. She smells nice, like lavender. I've been around Jenni hundreds of times before, but this feels intimate somehow. And now I'm noticing everything about Jenni. Her dark hair, shining in the diner lights. Her determined eyes as she cleans. Her soft lips.

I shake off the thoughts. I can't think of Jenni like this.

She dabs at my right leg, and Ronnie growls behind her. "I think you've got it, Jenni."

He looks at me like it's my fault that his sister was putting her hands on the right side of my lap. It wasn't like she was groping me or anything.

"Sorry, I was just trying to make it better," she stammers, her cheeks turning pink.

Dolores rushes up to our table with a rag. "I got this." She wipes up the mess, napkins and all. Once she has it cleaned up, she says, "I'll bring you out another Coke right away."

"Thanks, Dolores."

"I really am sorry," Jenni apologizes again.

"It's okay. Don't worry about it." I dab at my shirt with some more napkins I found from the little holder. The napkin is torn from Jenni's assault on the poor innocent napkin container.

"You two are so cute together." Dolores shows up with my Coke.

"Who? Me and Langston?" Jenni's laugh is clear like a bell. "We're practically siblings."

That shouldn't bother me. But for some reason it does.

"You don't look like siblings to me," Dolores says with a disbelieving glance in our direction. "There's something going on between the two of you. Mark my words."

A threatening look comes over Ronnie's features. "Langston and my sister? That better not be true." He glances over at my dad. "No offense, Mr. Keith. There's nothing wrong with your son or anything. It's just she's my sister and—"

Dad only laughs. "None taken. I have sisters too, so I understand. But the truth of the matter is, your sister will end up with someone one day, and there's nothing you'll be able to do to stop it."

Ronnie sticks his fingers in his ears. "La la la la la. I can't hear you."

I laugh. "You have nothing to worry about, bro. There's nothing between Jenni and me. We're just friends."

Why is it that Jenni's mouth dropped when I said that?

She couldn't possibly be unhappy about that statement, could she? I look back at her, and she's smiling. Maybe it was just my imagination.

"Do you two want to join us?" Dad offers.

"I would say yes, but there doesn't seem to be enough room for us here," Jenni says.

"Well, she could just snuggle up right next to Langston," Weston teases.

I fight off the heat that's creeping across my face.

"I can get you seated at a bigger table," Dolores offers.

"Good, because the seat is sticky now." I noticed it earlier when I put my hand on the vinyl next to me.

Soon, we are settled at the big table at the back, Jenni seated across the table, frustratingly far away.

"Jenni," Dad says once our burgers arrive, "I heard you're planning to race Valentine again."

"Yes, the doctor just cleared him."

"Better watch out, Langston," Weston teases.

"Why does everyone keep telling me that?" I grab a fry and bite off the end of it. All the fancy restaurants in the world, and we love coming to Harvey's. Nothing compares.

"Because she's going to win, man. Valentine is a champion," Ronnie says.

"And so is Thunder. He's been undefeated for three months now." I'm not scared of Jenni's horse. Okay, maybe I'm a little more nervous about it. I tug on my shirt. The soda is causing it to stick to my chest, and it's still cold and uncomfortable. I'm sure I smell great too. Unlike Jenni.

Where did that thought come from? I glance over

at Jenni. She's putting in her order for a chicken sandwich and a salad. The pantsuit she's wearing is tailored perfectly. Jenni is one of those girls who's always wearing the newest trends from top designers. She has an entire team of personal shoppers. The woman is drop-dead gorgeous.

Not that I'm staring or anything.

Except that I am.

I'm far from being like a brother to her, but I'm not going to let anyone know that. There's another reason that I spend most of my time in Blue Mountain. And it's not just because I enjoy the view.

I've barely even acknowledged it to myself. But tonight, having her so near to me, smelling of lavender, it's hard to deny that Jenni is a girl worth sticking around town for.

3

JENNI

*M*y cat, Noodle, bats at the tassels on my boots as my mom launches into the reasons why I need a husband. It's annoying. The speech, not the cat. Noodles is a troublemaker, but I adore him and he can do no wrong in my eyes.

"We're never going to have any grandchildren at this rate," my mom says for the zillionth time. They've been in this competition with the Keiths for years to see who can have the most grandchildren. So far, my parents are losing, since Weston and Callie have Angel.

My parents were star-crossed lovers. My mom is from India, and her family is very traditional and comes from old money. She was supposed to have this arranged marriage, but my mom, being the rebel that she is, fell in love with my dad instead, an American from Georgia. I don't know why her parents were so mad. It's not like my dad grew up on the wrong side of the tracks. He also comes from old money.

My grandpa on my dad's side grew up with Langston's grandpa, who were both in commercial real estate, and the family stayed best friends over the years.

Except for Langston and me. I wouldn't really say we were friends. More like rivals. Especially now that Valentine will be racing against Thunder again.

My mom's speech makes me feel like utter garbage, but I don't let her know that. At least not the reason it makes me feel bad. "Mom, you know I'm too focused on my career to have a boyfriend. How am I supposed to be a wife?"

My dad, Ronald Albert Finley the Fourth, owns Finley and Everly, a commercial real estate corporation that has been passed down the Finley male line for generations. I've been working for him since I was a teen, and he's been grooming me to take over as the VP of the company. Ronnie would be the CEO once Dad decides to retire.

So my declaration that I don't have time to date is pretty accurate. They're well aware of that. But that doesn't mean they don't want to be grandparents.

Noodle jumps up into my lap and purrs. I stroke his orange fur and allow him to calm me. Hearing my parents lecture me on being single is one of my least favorite activities.

"You're thirty years old now," my mom goes on. "It's time to settle down."

"Thirty is still plenty young," I say. "Lots of people don't get married until they're close to forty."

"By then, you'll be too old to have babies."

"Can we change the subject?" I request. The truth is, I can't have babies, but I haven't had the courage to tell my parents.

"You're always wanting to change the subject." Mom throws her hands in the air in frustration.

"Meera, maybe we should let it go for now." Dad puts a hand on her arm.

She pulls her hand away. "I don't want to let it go. Do you know what kind of pressure I'm under? Getting calls from my mother and my sisters always asking when my children are going to get married. All of my sisters are grandmothers now. Not to mention the Keiths gloating over the fact that they have Angel."

"Maybe you should try talking to Ronnie. He's perfectly capable of giving you grandchildren." As far as I know, anyway. They won't be getting any from me. Unless I decide to become a foster parent. It's something that's been on my mind a lot lately. It's a way I can help the community. Give some troubled kids a better life.

"We've tried talking to Ronnie about getting married. He's just as hardheaded as you are." Frustration laces her words.

"He has no excuse." Now I sound like my mom, but that's not an unusual thing. I catch myself sounding like her a lot. I adore her. We're usually so close, but this is the one topic we can't see eye to eye on, and it's killing me inside. I just can't bring myself to tell her the truth. I've known for a year now, and she hasn't hounded me too badly about the getting married thing, but ever since three of my cousins got pregnant in India, she's been harping on me nonstop.

It's really put a wedge between us.

"Do you guys want something to eat?" I offer, hoping food will be enough to get their minds off the marriage topic. "I made peanut butter cookies."

"You baked?" Mom looks shocked.

"I figured it couldn't be too hard."

That's enough to distract her, all right. She gets up and heads to the kitchen. My house is a new construction. I moved into it a year ago. It's crisp and white and airy with lots of tall windows that overlook the rolling hills and tree-covered mountains. I love nature, and I wanted to be able to see as much of it as I can.

I've wanted to learn to cook for a while, but I've found that I'm not especially good at it. I might ask my chef to give me lessons if my own attempts keep failing.

I lead them to the cooling rack sitting on the white marble countertop. My mom picks up a cookie and sniffs it like she's checking for poison. Then she hesitantly takes a bite, which crunches so loudly it practically echoes off the kitchen walls. She chews, and her eyes seem to water a little bit like she's in pain. She swallows and forces a smile.

"Do you want one, Dad?" I offer.

"Oh, thank you for the offer, but I'm back on my diet again." He pats his ample belly.

I narrow my eyes at him. "I saw you eating a big slice of pie last night."

"The diet started just... this morning."

"These can't be that bad." I grab a cookie and take a bite. I immediately run to the garbage and spit it out. "That was disgusting. I swear I followed all the directions."

"I think you forgot the sugar and maybe added a bit too much salt," Mom says.

"I put in what they said. A *T* of salt."

"Was that a big *T* or a little *T*?" Mom asks.

"I don't know. What's the difference? A *T* is a *T*."

Mom laughs. "Maybe you should think about taking some culinary classes. Or leave the cooking to Jacques," she says, referring to the chef I'd hired.

I sigh in frustration. Another failed recipe. I'm a smart, successful businesswoman. You would think I could figure out something simple like baking.

"What if she went on a date with Langston?" my dad says, switching back to our previous subject. He's been fairly quiet throughout Mom's tirade, and I get the impression that he's been thinking about it throughout the exchange about the cookies.

"Langston?" I shake my head. "He thinks of me as the annoying little sister."

"See? I told you, Ronald. She won't listen about him." Mom's voice is full of frustration. "I've always wanted our two families joined in marriage, but Jenni won't have it."

"More like Langston won't have it," I say to defend myself. "He's probably still hung up on Sarah." After having his ex-wife, Amanda, leave him, and then his ex-girlfriend, Sarah, leave as well, I'd imagine Langston is pretty burnt out on women.

"Oh no. I know the scoop on that from talking to Laurie," she says, referring to Langston's mom, one of her very best friends. "He's ready to move on."

"How does she know that?" I can't believe that Langston's mom would have any idea of what's going on in his love life. Not really. She thinks she knows, but that's very different from actually knowing what's going on in Langston's heart. He's not one to open up about that kind of stuff.

"Well, a mother knows these things about her child."

Right... Just like Mom knows all my secrets...

"Well, if we can get Langston to agree to take you on a date, would you be willing to go?" Dad asks.

"What? Are you going to bribe him or something?" What could they possibly bribe him with? The guy already has more money than he could ever spend.

"If you're not willing to date Langston or any of the men we've already tried setting you up with, I'm going to start asking my family if they know of any eligible bachelors in India for you."

I shudder. That's the last thing I want, all my aunts getting together, setting me up with some guy I don't know. At least I'd know what I was getting with Langston. "Fine. If Langston agrees to take me on a date, I'll go with him."

My mom gets this look in her eyes, like I've just given her a gift on Christmas morning. "You would do that?"

"Sure. It's just Langston." I shrug. Nothing will ever come of it. I know that for a fact.

My mom squeals. "Just wait until I tell Laurie. Our dream is finally coming true. A Finley and a Keith together at last."

"Whoa, whoa, whoa. Don't get ahead of yourself. It's just a date, and he hasn't even agreed to it yet."

"Oh, he will. I'll make sure of that."

"Mom. You can't bully the guy into taking me out."

"But I can win him over with sweets." She eyes me. "But we'll leave the cooking to Ruby."

I grin. "Are you saying I'll just chase him off with my cooking?"

She folds her arms and looks at me. "I'm not saying anything."

But I'm no dummy.

~

"*W*hat are you doing here?" I ask Langston as he approaches me at my parents' stable. Valentine has finished with the trainer, who's just packed up and left. "Coming to spy on the competition?" I tease. "Afraid you can't win on your own merits?"

"No. I was just looking for Ronnie." Langston is wearing a cowboy hat, plaid shirt, jeans, and cowboy boots. He looks like he's come straight from the pages of a western romance novel. I try not to think about the muscles under that shirt, either.

"Oh, in the mood to jump in the lake like a bunch of monkeys?" I think about that question for a minute and then say, "Actually, monkeys would be smarter than that. They know to avoid freezing cold water."

Langston's mouth quirks up. "You seemed to be enjoying it once you got in there."

"That was your imagination," I shoot back. "I hated every minute of it."

He laughs, one of my favorite sounds. Langston has a great laugh. It's full and rich and makes you want to laugh with him.

"So I might need a favor from you," I say. "Well, there's no might about it. I do need a favor from you."

He looks at me from under the brim of his cowboy hat. "Uh, oh. Should I be scared right now?"

"I can't really answer that for you," I say truthfully. "Don't take this the wrong way, okay?"

Langston crosses his arms and leans against the stable wall. "Fine. Now tell me what you want me to do."

"I need you to take me out on a date."

"Wow, you just said that with a straight face."

"That's...because I was serious."

"Ohhh. And why do you need me to take you out?"

I wipe back a strand of hair that escaped my bun. "Because I need to get my parents off my back. They're driving me nuts. My mom is threatening to match me up with a guy in India. Some dude I've never met."

"So I'm supposed to swoop in like the knight in shining armor?"

I wrinkle my nose. "Never say that again. You know I don't need saving."

"Oh, I think you do. You're the one asking for favors," Langston points out.

I groan. "Fine. I need your help. But this is me saving myself. Asking for a favor from a friend."

"A friend, huh?" Langston grins at me, both dimples popping. "That's quite the upgrade."

I give him a weird look. "What do you mean by upgrade?"

"Well, I wasn't even friend-zoned before this. I was in the doghouse," he explains, pulling out his phone and swiping at the screen.

"I think you're mixing up your metaphors," I say. "And pay attention. This is important."

He looks up from his phone. "I'm listening. I just had a weird text come in."

"Do you need to take care of something?" I ask.

He slips his phone into his pocket. "It can wait." He looks back up at me. "You were saying?"

"You think you're in the doghouse with me?"

"Well, yeah. We aren't exactly friendly with each other. You plan on decimating my horse in this next race."

"But you know I consider you a friend, right?" I don't know why this is suddenly so important to me.

"You just said that, so yes." Langston fiddles with his phone again.

Is he paying attention? "So about that date..."

"You're asking me on a date. How forward of you."

"We're not in the 1800s," I tease. "I think it's okay. Anyway, there's nothing romantic about it. Just a little help from a friend."

"I like how you upgraded me now that you need something," he teases back.

I pretend to be offended. "How rude!"

"But that being said... I'm willing to help you out."

"Why do I sense there's a catch here?" What am I getting myself into? I'm not so sure I should trust Langston. The guy plans to decimate my horse in the races, after all. He's the competition.

"No catch. But I want to reserve a favor for later."

I stare at him. Maybe this isn't such a good idea. Who knows what Langston would want? "Why later?"

He grins. "Because I haven't thought of anything I want yet."

I reach out and pet Marshmallow, who's been watching us from his stall. "So, when are you taking me out? And you might want to tell your mom that you're taking me out because I think my parents plan to gang up on us with your parents."

"Interesting. And sounds very familiar."

"How so?"

"My parents want me to date you as well. Something about joining the families." He shakes his hips. "Making babies."

I fake scowl at him. "Don't do that. It's just gross."

"Ouch. You hurt my feelings."

"Come on. We both know you have a heart of stone."

"That's because you don't know me." He leans closer to me.

"Oh, I know you. I've been around you our entire lives." My face flushes. Why is it doing that? I refuse to like Langston. I take a deep breath to cool my cheeks. Hopefully, he doesn't notice.

"You see the version of me you want to believe."

"I see what's in front of my face. Are you telling me you've been putting on some sort of act?" I refuse to get pulled in by him. Or even acknowledge anything that might be causing my heart to pound right now.

His phone rings. He looks down at it, and a fearful expression comes over his face for a slight second before he silences the call and puts his phone back into his pocket. "Sorry. It's been fun. I gotta go. Shoot me a text, and we can talk about our date."

I watch him leave. He never did find Ronnie. I guess I distracted him. What was going on between us anyway? I'm not sure what to think of it.

I brush Marshmallow's fur, thinking over what the trainer had said earlier about Valentine's progress in an attempt to shake off the... whatever it was between Langston and me earlier.

My parents' golden retriever, Goldie, wanders into the stable, her tail wagging and her belly heavy with puppies. I reach down and pet her head. Ronnie comes in after her.

"She looks like she's about due," I say.

"Any day now," Ronnie says. He glances over his shoulder. "What was Langston all upset about?"

"I'm not sure. He was acting funny a minute ago.

He said something about a weird text." I shrug and pat Marshmallow's white head.

"I heard Mom and Dad want you to date him."

"We're going on a date."

"You and Langston?" Ronnie growls. "You don't know everything about him, Jenni."

I feel defensive right away. "Mom's going to try to set me up with some stranger in India. How would that be better? She didn't do the arranged marriage thing. I'm not going to carry on that family tradition either."

"I don't think Langston is the guy for you."

"You're the only one then. Everyone else seems to think we're perfect for each other."

"That's because they don't know what I know."

"It doesn't matter anyway. I'm not dating him for real. It's just to get Mom and Dad off my back."

That seems to calm Ronnie down a bit. "Oh. That's different. But tell him not to get any big ideas, or he'll have to answer to me."

"Ooh scary."

"I mean it. I don't want you dating him."

"You can't tell me who to date." Now I'm mad. "Langston is your best friend. How can you talk about him like that? If you like him so much, wouldn't you want him dating me?"

"I know too much about him. Let's just leave it at that. You deserve better."

"You'd probably say that about any guy I wanted to date," I point out.

He grins. "You're probably right. But that's what makes me such a good brother."

"You're really annoying. You know that, right?"

He only laughs in return.

4

LANGSTON

I haven't heard from her in years. Talk about a blast from the past. Why would Amanda be reaching out to me? Once I'm in my car, I read and re-read the text I got from her while I was in the stables talking to Jenni.

Amanda: Langston. I haven't been fully honest with you. Is there a time we could talk in person soon?

I put the car into reverse and drive home. What would Amanda possibly have to tell me after all these years? We would have been married ten years by now if she'd decided to stay married.

It's concerning that she wants to talk in person too. Whatever she has to tell me must be huge. When I pull into my garage, I shoot her a text.

Langston: I'm in Blue Mountain these days. You're welcome to come here.

I'm trying to think of the best way to meet. It's not like she can stay with me. Maybe my parents' house? She's been to their house many times, but that's not very private either. Who knows what my mom would think about Amanda showing up on their doorstep? Would she be rooting for us to get back together?

Amanda: I can be there next week.

Langston: Are you sure you can't just tell me over the phone? I'd hate for you to go through all the trouble of traveling here if it can be handled over a call.

Amanda: You'll understand when I get there. Let's just say I have my reasons...

Now I'm extra curious.

Langston: How did you get my number?

Amanda: It's the same one you've had all this time.

Langston: You kept it?

Amanda: I thought I might need to talk to you one day.

I pocket my phone and head into the house, closing the garage door before going into the kitchen. My dog, Sausage, comes waddling over to me. He's a little dachshund who is obsessed with eating. As a result, his belly hangs so low it practically drags on the ground. His pointy little tail hits my legs as he barks his greeting.

It's not my fault he's so fat. I can't help it that he loves food so much. I can't deny him anything. Just one look at that face he makes, and I give in. Okay, so maybe it's my fault. Partially. I don't force him to take all the food I offer.

"You need to go on a diet, Sausage."

But he and I both know that won't actually happen.

"You need to stop feeding that dog so much." Stella comes into the room with a cleaning rag in her hand. She and I have gotten to be good friends over the years, and we tease each other. Stella is dating one of my landscapers and sometimes we exchange relationship advice. She was there for me when I broke up with Sarah.

Without Stella, my chef, Powell, and my personal assistant, Maggie, I don't know how I'd survive.

"I can't help it that he's always hungry." Then I get a bright idea. "Maybe you could start taking him on walks for me. If you're open to putting in more hours."

"I don't mind doing that." Stella grins.

"I could take him out too. I need to spend more time with the little guy." I bend down to scratch behind his ears. "I get the feeling you won't like it though. Huh, Sausage?"

The funny thing about his name is that we can't feed him any sausage, or he gets sick. I learned that the hard way early on when I thought I was being cute by feeding him what he's named after. But he sure looks like a sausage. A bulging one.

Sausage is a special dog though. He's been there for me over the years. Like when I broke up with Sarah, he would just sit by my side and be there. It was like he sensed I was sad, and he wanted to help me feel better.

"Should we take you out for a walk right now?" Stella asks the little guy.

He barks in response, waddling his little legs around in excitement, his tail snapping between my two legs.

"He's more excited than I expected," I say.

Stella goes to get his leash, and I text my stable manager, letting him know I'd like to ride Dash for a bit so he can get him saddled up, and then I head out back toward the stable. I walk out there as dusk begins to fall. The sun is setting over the mountains, shooting ribbons of orange across the lawn.

I hear barking behind me, and I turn to see Stella coming toward us. "He wants to follow you."

"He can take a walk out to the stables if he wants," I say.

His belly drags across the ground, leaving a trail of bent grass behind him. A car engine roars, and I look over to see Ronnie driving up in his red convertible. He pulls up to the stable, which I've almost reached, and gets out of his car. "Hey, I heard you were looking for me," he says.

"I'll just take Sausage to the street to walk." Stella tugs him in the opposite direction, glancing at Ronnie, like she senses we need privacy. Sausage doesn't seem to like it though.

"Go on, silly dog. Get some exercise. It's good for you."

Stella laughs, and finally Sausage gives up his fight and allows her to lead him toward the road.

"That dog has gotten fat," Ronnie says.

I laugh. "Yeah. We're starting him on a new walking regimen because I'm weak, and I can't stop letting him have snacks."

"So what did you want to tell me?" Ronnie asks.

I walk into the stable toward Dash. "Did you hear that my dad is looking for a new company to merge with? He's thinking of merging with this big company in Singapore, but they're being difficult."

"Isn't that stuff top secret?" Ronnie jokes.

"Keep it between us, of course."

"I was only kidding. You know I wouldn't repeat something like that to the wrong people."

"But if it's true, I may end up going to Singapore a lot more."

"I thought Ashton was handling the Singapore division." We stop in front of Dash's stall.

"He is. But there will be a lot more to do over there, and there's a lot of schmoozing we'll need to do."

"Didn't your parents just buy a resort in Singapore?" Ronnie pets Dash's black mane.

"Well, it's off the coast. An entire island that they're developing into a resort. That's where Kaison proposed to Ariana."

Ronnie lifts his brows. "Wow. Impressive move on his part."

"I know. It'll be hard to outdo that."

"Speaking of..." Ronnie's not smiling anymore. "I heard you're planning to take Jenni out on a date."

"Yeah, so what?" I cross my arms and keep strong. I can't let Ronnie know how nervous I am about him hearing about this.

"I don't really like the idea. You're my best friend. You know I love you. But that doesn't mean I want you hitting on my sister either. Not after the way you betrayed me."

"What do you mean by that?"

"Amanda." Ronnie has his arms crossed now too, matching my stance. "You knew I was into her, and you swooped in and took her anyway."

"If you're so into Amanda, she's all yours." I have no interest in ever getting her back.

"The point is, if you can't be loyal to me, what makes me think you won't treat my sister the same?"

"It's just a date. Relax. I have no intention of hurting Jenni. She asked me to go on a date with her as friends to get your parents off her back. Your mom's threatened to match her up with a guy in India she's never met."

"So it's a fake date?" He gets quiet for a moment. "I don't think I like that any better. What if her feelings get involved, and then you just ghost her?"

"She's the one begging me to take her out. She barely tolerates me. The last thing that's going to happen is something romantic between Jenni and me."

He scowls at me. "Somehow, that doesn't make me feel better."

"Well, I can't make both of you happy," I say in frustration.

"I don't see why she can't try dating someone in India," Ronnie says.

"Are you serious? That's a horrible idea. Are you saying that because she'll end up with a guy your parents have handpicked?"

"It's not a bad idea."

Jake, my stable manager, has Dash all saddled up for me. He used to be a racehorse a few years back, but he's retired now. We had to spend quite a bit of effort to get him trained to become a trail horse, since racehorses are so unruly for the average person to ride. His official racing name was "Dash from the Box." The names we register our horses as can't be used by anyone else, so many of the registered names are long and strange and end up with barn names we use at home. Usually, it's something totally different, but with Dash, we just shortened it.

Valentine's registered name is "Love comes Quickly" and Thunder's is "Ahead of the Storm."

"Do you want to ride too?" I ask Ronnie. He's wearing jeans and a t-shirt and boots.

"Sure."

Without having to be asked, Jake grabs a saddle and proceeds to put it on Dragon, Ronnie's favorite horse.

"Are you ready for the race tomorrow?" Ronnie asks.

"I have a good feeling about this new jockey," I say.

"You got a new jockey?" Ronnie looks surprised.

"Yeah. I didn't tell you?"

Ronnie gives me a suspicious look. "This doesn't have to do with the fact that Jenni has Valentine racing again, does it?"

"Hey, I'm just trying to keep my edge."

"You were doing great with your other jockey. Why switch it up?"

"You know why."

Ronnie grins. "Why don't you tell me?"

Ugh. I don't want to. "Because Valentine beat Thunder with the old jockey, and I feel the need to switch it up," I mumble.

"I'm sorry, what was that? Did you say it's because you're scared Valentine will beat Thunder?" Ronnie teases.

"Whose side are you on, anyway?" I mount Dash and grab the reins.

Jake finishes up saddling Dragon, and then Ronnie swings into the saddle.

"Valentine's, of course."

"Traitor."

Ronnie throws his head back and laughs, and we head out on the trail I have on my property. My phone buzzes in my front pocket, but I don't pull it out. "Going back to the Amanda topic. She just reached out to me today."

We head into the woods, down a trail.

"No kidding. What did she want?"

I fill him in on the details of my exchange with Amanda. I know Amanda is a sore spot between us, so I tread lightly. But if she's going to be in town, he needs to be prepared.

We come out of the woods into a clearing that overlooks the little town of Blue Mountain nestled among the hills, and we stop and take in the view. My house is situated up the hill from the Finleys' property and my parents' place as well. I can see the lake where we were swimming and the Finley's main house on the other side of a patch of woods. My parents' historic home peeks at us through the trees and their horses grazing in the clearing look like tiny toys from here.

"My phone buzzed while we were on the trail just now." I pull it out of my front pocket since we're stopped.

"Is it a text from her?" Ronnie leans over like he'd be able to see the text from where he is.

"No, this one is from my mom. It looks like

Amanda has reached out to her and asked her if she could stay at her place."

"Oh, great. Your mom is involved now. This ought to be fun."

I grit my teeth. "Yeah. A total blast. Woohoo." I spin a finger in the air.

"Do you think she's after more money? She could have gotten a lot more out of you than she did when you divorced, and maybe she's interested in patching things up to get more."

"I didn't even think of that. You know what my biggest fear is here?" I say. "It's my mom. What if she tries to push me to patch things up with Amanda?"

"You think your mom would do that?"

"She was just talking about how she thought I could have tried harder to save our marriage. She's desperate for a grandkid." I prod Dash forward, and we fly down the hill to the pasture. There's a reason this horse used to race. His powerful legs tear into the ground as his hooves pound across the grass.

Dragon's hoof-beats sound behind me, and I slow Dash to a walk. He falls in line beside me. I have a race-track set up on my property for my racehorses to practice on. Since no one is using it right now, I lead him over to it and enjoy a few laps with the air hitting my face and ruffling through my hair.

The more I think about Amanda coming into town, the more appealing that date with Jenni sounds. I don't expect it to go anywhere, but I don't want Amanda getting any bright ideas about turning into a gold-digger either.

Maybe I'm being too harsh on her. She could have gotten a lot more money out of me when we split. But I've had a lot of women after me for my money, so a little caution comes with the territory. I keep a social media page, and it's the worst there. Women begging me to marry them in the comments.

Sarah wasn't a gold-digger, at least. But she didn't want to take our relationship to the distance either. She left me for another guy who ended up cheating on her a few months later. I heard through my mom, who stalks Sarah on social media, that Sarah is dating someone again. I don't follow Sarah on any platforms, so I wouldn't have heard. Not from my own snooping, anyway.

"I thought your parents were all excited for you to date Jenni, anyway," Ronnie says.

"They don't know I'm taking her on a date."

His mouth curves downward. "You know I don't like that."

"It's nothing serious, but it might help keep Amanda in check."

"You mean, pretend Jenni is your girlfriend around Amanda?" Ronnie asks.

"Something like that." If it makes Ronnie feel better that I'm fake dating Jenni, then he can think that. I don't plan to make any moves on Jenni, but she's a gorgeous woman. And this might be a way to get Ronnie to calm down about me taking her out.

~

I open my front door to see my mom on my front step. "What's this about Amanda coming to see us?"

"You get right to the point, don't you, Mom?" I widen the door to let her in.

She bustles past. "Of course, I told her she could stay with us. She was a good daughter-in-law to us. I still can't understand why she ever left in the first place." She makes a beeline for my living room. "Do you think she wants you back?"

I sink into the sofa next to the loveseat where she's plopped herself.

"I have no idea. All I know is she acts like she wants to see me in person for some reason."

"She's being so secretive. Do you want me to have someone look into it for you?"

I raise an eyebrow. "Like a detective?"

"You know we have people that can dig up info. Your dad has connections."

"I don't need his connections. I don't want Amanda investigated. That would be weird. We can just let her speak her mind when she gets here."

Mom gets this pouty look on her face, and she crosses her arms. "I don't like waiting."

"Well, it won't be long. She should be here in a week."

"I couldn't believe it when she called me," Mom says. "I was so shocked."

"You and me both. She was the last person I was expecting to hear from."

"Do you think she wants to get back together?" Mom asks.

"That's what I'm worried about. The Amanda ship has sailed, and I'm long over it. To be honest, she never was right for me to begin with. We were young and jumped into the relationship too quickly. Amanda had too many emotional issues she needed to work out anyway. She wasn't ready for marriage."

"But it's possible she's gotten help and fixed those issues now." Mom is getting this hopeful look on her face.

"No way. I'm not interested in her. She ran away once. What's to keep her from running away again after taking a bunch of our money?"

"She didn't take any money last time, and she was entitled to it," Mom points out.

"And I think she's coming back to collect."

"She never seemed to like you for your money before," Mom says. "If anything, she turned her nose up at us for having more than others."

"Come on, Mom. She was entitled to millions. You don't think she wants her money?"

"She can't get it now anyway," Mom argues. "Not unless you marry her again. I know you're saying you don't want to reopen that chapter of your past, but what if there's happiness waiting for you there?"

Panic races through me. I have to do something, and fast, to keep my mom from heading down this road.

And I know exactly what needs to happen.

5

JENNI

"Noodle, get out of the noodles." And this is where she got her name. When I rescued her from the local animal shelter, I had a bowl of noodles I was about to eat, and she buried her tiny head in it and started chowing down.

This crazy cat will eat noodles right out of my hand and loves to bat at them. She's like a little orange mini tiger too, always attacking things. She likes to perch up high and look over the house like it's her personal kingdom, so I got her a massive kitty playground. It may or may not be taking up half my family room in the basement. That entire space is dedicated to Noodle. I figure if I can't fill my house with children, I can at least give Noodle the best life possible.

I walk over to where Noodle is feasting on a

container of leftover spaghetti I needed to put back in the fridge from my cooking lesson earlier.

My doorbell rings, and I go to open it to find Langston standing on the front step.

"What's up?" I open the door wider for him to come in.

He walks by me. "Were you serious about that date?"

"Yes, very. I need to get my mom off my back."

"Good. Because I might need more than one date from you."

A laugh falls from my mouth. "What?"

"It wouldn't be real, of course."

"Of course." But for some reason that bugs me. Why should I care that he doesn't want it to be real? I don't even want to think about that can of worms. "So why the urgency all of a sudden?"

"Well, Amanda is coming into town, and I don't want her to think I'm available."

"Let's go sit down," I say. "This is a longer conversation than I thought it would be."

He follows me into the kitchen where Noodle is curled up in one of his many cat beds.

"You hungry?" I ask. "I would offer you some of the spaghetti I made earlier, but Noodle got into it."

Langston grins. "Sounds appetizing."

Noodle looks up at Langston and meows.

"You've spoiled her with all the treats you've given her when you come over here."

"I thought you said she just ate."

"You would think she'd be full, but I guess she saved room for whatever she thinks you might be offering this time." It's usually a piece of deli meat or a tiny chunk of chicken.

Noodle rubs against Langston's leg and meows again, this time in a more demanding tone.

Langston opens my fridge and pulls out a package of ham.

"Just make yourself comfortable, why don't you?"

"Don't mind if I do." Langston grins and pulls out some meat for Noodle. She stands on her hind legs and greedily bites it from his fingers.

"You're spoiling her rotten."

"I'm pretty sure from looking at that giant kitty paradise in your basement that I'm not the one to blame here."

I laugh. "I don't know what you're talking about."

"Getting back to the date thing..."

I settle onto a couch in the living area connected to the kitchen. My place has an open concept. Langston sits next to me.

"So you want to take me on a bunch of fake dates."

"Well, I need you to pretend to be my girlfriend actually."

"Oh, we're taking this deception to a whole other level. I don't know how I feel about that."

"Think of it this way. It'll get your parents off your back, my parents off my back, and keep Amanda at bay."

"Why is Amanda coming into town? Are you guys getting back together?"

"Not if I have anything to do with it. She texted me and said she wants to talk to me and that it has to happen in person. My guess is she feels like she didn't get enough out of me at our divorce settlement and is coming back for more. My mom is delighted to have her around and offered to let her stay at their place."

"So she contacted you and said something about money?" I'm having trouble figuring out how all this came to pass.

"She didn't say specifically that it's about money. That's just a speculation on my part. But she was being cryptic. The bottom line is I'm worried my mom will try to push me to get back together with her."

"What's wrong with her?" I tease. "She's not your type?"

His face goes dark. "She left our marriage. I don't really want to talk about it."

"So you want me to pretend to date you?"

"Yes."

"I don't know if that's such a great idea. I don't want

everyone getting their hopes up that we're going to last. It wouldn't be fair to them."

"I guess you could always explore your options in India then." A smile is playing at the corners of his lips.

"On second thought…"

He laughs. "Yeah. That's what I thought. So, are we doing this then?"

I sigh. "It's not ideal."

"But what is ideal about this situation anyway?"

He has a good point.

Noodle jumps up on the couch and stares Langston down hard.

"I'm all out of meat, kitty." He shows her his empty hands, but she meows demandingly at him.

I can't help but laugh.

Noodle eventually gives up and snuggles beside Langston.

"I guess you've won her loyalty," I say.

"That's what happens when you spoil a kitty."

"So back to the fake dating thing," I say. "How is this going to work? Are we going to have to kiss each other and stuff?"

Langston smiles. "Isn't that what couples do?"

"Not always in public. Some people don't like PDA."

"But we're putting on a show, and we need it to be convincing. My mom can sniff out lies like a bloodhound. After raising five boys, she's become quite the expert."

I laugh. "You guys did put her through a lot growing up, so it's no surprise."

"We broke so many things in the house and blamed them on each other."

I shake my head with a smile. "Typical boys. Ronnie tried to do that to me too, but our parents always believed me."

"And sometimes it was you," Langston pointed out. "More often than not."

I keep a straight face. "Whatever. I was a perfect angel growing up. I never broke any rules."

"Oh right. Like the time your mom said all the cookies were for the ladies at the knitting club, and you ate most of them and then blamed it on Ronnie and me."

"I'm sure you're remembering that wrong. I wouldn't have done such a thing," I tease.

"And the stomachache you were complaining about for the rest of the day or the fact that you wouldn't touch your dinner had nothing to do with it?"

I smack him on the arm playfully. "How do you remember all this stuff?"

"I remember everything."

"I'm not so sure that's a good thing," I say.

"Why? Because it means you can't try to rewrite the

past to your benefit?" He's laughing now, and I join him. He knows me all too well.

"I would never do that..."

"Sure, little Miss Innocent," Langston says. "So, back to the PDA stuff. What will it be? Holding hands? Kissing?"

"Fine. If the situation arises that we need to kiss, then we can. But it has to be something simple, like a kiss on the cheek."

"On the cheek? They're not going to buy that."

"Fine," I relent. "A quick peck on the lips."

Langston grins at me. "And holding hands too?"

"Of course," I say. "So, when will our first date be?"

"Can I get back to you on that?"

"Yes. But you're being weird."

"I just have a crazy idea, that's all. And it needs to be big if we're going to convince everyone that we're actually dating. We'll report back to them and everything."

I laugh. "Okay."

"But I'm thinking it will involve a flight to Atlanta, so you'll want to clear your entire day."

"I don't see why it needs to be such a big ordeal. We could go to the coffee shop or something."

"Do you want to convince your mom that we're together or not?"

"I think she'll see right through whatever you have planned."

"Nope. She definitely won't. But you'll have to prepare yourself. It's awfully romantic. You might fall for me for real." He waggles his brows at me.

I bark out a surprised laugh. "Not on your life."

He grins. "Am I really so repulsive?"

"No..." I backtrack. "You're just Langston, Ronnie's best friend—and the enemy."

Langston laughs. "You're just mad that Thunder's been winning so much lately."

"I'm not mad... But I see it like it is, too."

~

I finish the water in my crystal glass and set it aside and glance out the window at the trees beneath us.

I'm wearing a flowy tan blouse and white jeans. My hair has been straightened. I don't know why I bothered. It's just Langston. But I do like dressing up, so this is for me, not him.

Langston is wearing a white shirt and tie, his suit jacket casually draped over the seat next to him. I'm sure he's wearing that suit for himself too...

Annie, our flight attendant, comes up to us. "Would you like me to take your jacket, Mr. Keith?"

"That would be great." Langston picks it up and hands it to her.

She takes it from him and smiles. "Is there

anything else I can get you? A refill on your drink, perhaps?"

He looks at the crystal flute of champagne and hands it to her. "Not at this time."

"Yes, sir."

She turns to me. "Ms. Finley? Can I get you anything else before we land?"

"No, thank you." I'm saving room for dinner.

We're barely in the air before it's time for us to land again. We arrive at a small airport in Atlanta. Not the big commercial one. Most families with private jets avoid that place like the plague. I have a headache just thinking about it.

"Don't you think this is a bit over the top?" I complain.

"Oh no. Heaven forbid I treat you to something fancy. Remember, the more over the top it is, the more your mom will buy into it."

"What if Ronnie tells them it's not real?" I ask. Langston told me Ronnie knows we're planning to fake date.

"He'd better not. I don't know why he'd do that, anyway."

"Isn't he going to get mad if our date ends up being romantic?"

"I'll let him know there's nothing actually going on between us, and he won't care," Langston explains.

There's a car waiting for us with our driver, Nate,

one of the Atlanta staff members that serves the Keith family. We've done so many things together for so many years that we all know the employees that work for the families.

The air is cool, and I wish I'd brought a jacket. But Nate has the car warm, and I slide into the back seat. I scoot all the way over to make room for Langston.

"Where are we going?" I ask when Nate pulls out of the airport.

"You'll see."

We drive through traffic and eventually pull up to the Fox Theater. "Are we watching a show? What about dinner?"

"Don't worry, I won't let you go hungry. Heaven forbid you get hangry on me."

I roll my eyes. "I don't get hangry..."

"You don't? Then why do you have daggers shooting out of your eyes when it takes too long for our food to come out at the diner?"

I scowl at him. "I don't want to talk about it."

Nate opens my door, and I get out. Langston opens his own door and steps out of the car. "I had to pull some last-minute strings, but I have connections at the theater."

We go inside, and I'm expecting a crowd, but the place is deserted. "Are you sure you didn't get the times mixed up or something?" It's two in the afternoon on a Tuesday, so it's not unusual for the theater to be empty.

"I bought out the theater for us."

"You what?" It's like he's joking, but there's no one here but us.

A theater employee greets us at the ticket counter. "Welcome to Fox Theater! If you'll follow me, I'll show you to your seats." She's peppy with her dark hair back in a bun, but I get the feeling she spends some time on the stage as well as running the ticket booth.

I took a couple acting classes for fun in high school. My parents hired a private acting coach, and I was in a couple of shows. I haven't done anything theater-related in years.

"You remembered that I love musicals?" I say.

"I told you, I remember everything." Langston offers me his arm, and we walk to the front of the theater.

I look down at his arm. "Is this really necessary?" I whisper.

"You're supposed to be playing along," he whispers back to me.

I don't want to admit this to Langston, but this is actually pretty cool. I've been too busy with work to stop to have some fun. Other than riding Marshmallow, that is. I will always make time for him.

There's a table and chairs set up just below the front row. The table is covered with a white tablecloth, and there are candles burning. There's an entire orchestra sitting in the pit, waiting for us. The curtains are closed.

We settle in our chairs, and Langston pulls out his phone. "We need documentation of this moment. You know, so we can spread the word that we're together."

I lean in closer to get in the shot, close enough that I can smell the aftershave on Langston's neck. It's not actually gross either. He smells...nice.

I look down and see the program has been sitting next to me the entire time, and I haven't even noticed it. *Les Misérables*. My favorite musical. I hadn't even heard it was playing. But I've been so wrapped up in racing Valentine that I haven't paid attention to what was going on in the theater world in Atlanta.

"You got us a private viewing of *Les Mis*?"

"Don't get too excited about it. I didn't plan it that way. That's just what was playing this week."

"Oh, I thought maybe you were doing something sweet and thoughtful for a minute."

"Hey, this dinner should count as sweet and thoughtful," he protests.

"And it does. Ten points to Langston for being creative."

"Only ten? This is a good date. It should be more like twenty or thirty."

"We'll see how good dinner is, and then maybe you'll be up to twenty."

He shakes his head with a smile.

The lights dim and the curtains part as the music begins to play. Our food is brought out during the first act and is from the Indian restaurant my family loves to go to when we're in Atlanta. It's better than my parents' cook even, and she's a master at preparing Indian dishes.

During intermission, I get up to go to the bathroom, and Langston checks his phone.

"Two missed calls from Amanda."

"I wonder what she wants," I say.

"You're not the only one," Langston says, following me out of the theater.

"You know, this is the best fake date I've ever been on," I tell him.

"Thank you. So did I do good then?"

"Meh," I say through a smile.

Langston grins. "You were impressed. Just admit it."

I can't help but smile too. "I might have been a *little* impressed. But don't think that will happen on a regular basis or anything," I add quickly before he gets the wrong idea.

We get to the bathrooms and split up. The truth is, I'm blown away by the date Langston planned. I wasn't expecting it, and now I'm not sure how I feel about it. Who knew he could be so romantic? And is there some part of him that wants it to all be real?

6

LANGSTON

Today is race day, and my stomach is tied in knots as I head to the Blue Mountain Racetrack. The Finleys and Keiths created this race-track years ago, and we've been holding races here for generations. I keep reminding myself that I've done everything I can to prepare and I have to let Thunder and his jockey do their jobs. I take a seat as the race begins. Jenni is sitting with her family nearby. I look over to see her all dressed up with a fancy hat and everything. We go all out when it's racing day.

"How was your date with Jenni?" my mom asks when I take a seat next to her.

"It went well. I took her to see *Les Mis*."

"You know that's her favorite musical, right?"

"That's what I understand."

My mom's face glows with excitement. "I can hear those wedding bells already!"

Kaison leans forward. "Mom, he's not telling you the whole story. I heard he bought out the entire theater to give her a private showing."

"What? Langston, you sly dog! Who knew you were such a romantic?" Ashton says, punching me in the arm. He flew back from Singapore to see the race when he heard Valentine was cleared by the vet.

"I already knew that." Mom waves her phone in the air. "I saw it on social media." She turns to me. "You must really like Jenni if you're treating her that way."

"Either that or he wants something," Kaison says.

"You hush. I don't need that kind of negativity right now," Mom scolds, swatting him on the arm. She turns to me.

Kaison only laughs at her.

Dad shows up with a hot dog and a large Coke and settles next to Mom. "What are we talking about?"

"Langston rented out the entire Fox Theater to impress Jenni. I just have to talk to Meera about this!" My scheming mother stands up and heads over to where the Finleys are sitting.

"That's not embarrassing or anything," I mutter under my breath.

"You have no idea how bad she was before Ariana and I got together. She was practically begging us to join in holy matrimony," Kaison says.

"Where is Ariana today?" I ask.

"She's having a girls' day out with her cousin."

"I'm surprised she was able to stand a moment away from you. Every time I'm around you two, I get nauseated from watching you suck face," I say.

"So what about you and Jenni? Was there any face sucking going on?" Ashton asks with a devilish grin.

"None of your business." I glance over at Jenni and my cheeks grow hot. The truth is, I barely even touched her, other than linking arms. She looked gorgeous though. It's not that I didn't want to kiss her. I thought about it several times that night. But I'm not a fan of having my face punched either. She was pretty specific about her rules. I guess I could have gotten away with a peck, but what if it was good and it turned into more? If it ever got back to Ronnie that I was making out with his sister, it would be... Well, I don't even want to go there.

The truth is, Jenni had a good time that night. She was glowing by the time the night was over and was even nice to me a few times.

Mom returns to her seat all aflutter about her conversation with Meera, but I don't get to hear the details because the race is beginning.

I'm on the edge of my seat the entire time. I glance over to see Jenni with her hand to her mouth, her nails perfectly manicured. It's a moment of vulnerability I don't often see from her. Is she as nervous about winning as I am? Thunder has been on a winning streak, and I'm not excited to see that broken.

Thunder and Valentine are neck and neck for the majority of the race, and my heart is pounding as I squish the program in my clutched fist.

As they cross the finish line, it's too hard to tell who's won. But then Valentine is announced as the winner, and my jaw tightens and my teeth clench. Even all that extra time with the trainer, the new jockey, wasn't good enough. I want to throw my wrinkled-up program, but that would be littering, and I care about the planet.

"Better luck next time." Kaison pats me on the back.

"So much for that winning streak," Ashton says, shaking his head, sharing my disappointment.

I don't want their sympathy. I don't need it because this has taught me that I only need to work harder. I glance over to see Jenni celebrating with her family, and I scowl. To think I was starting to like her a little bit. I know I'm being a bad sport, but I want to let myself wallow for a minute before I have to face her.

"I don't know how I feel about this," Mom says. "I wanted Thunder to win, but I can't help but feel so happy for Jenni that Valentine is doing so well after his injury."

She's a better person than me. I'm grumpy about my loss.

As we're walking to the waiting car, Jenni falls into step next to me.

"You coming over here to gloat?" I ask, slowing my gait so the rest of the family walks away a bit so we can talk without them overhearing.

"Nope. You look sad enough all on your own."

"So you're saying you're happy when I'm sad? I thought you said we were friends now."

She nudges me with her elbow, which is kind of hot and borderline flirty, and my bad feeling dissipates a little. "That's not what I was saying at all. Don't put words in my mouth, silly. And we're still friends. Unless you're too much of a sore loser to handle a friendship with the girl who just decimated you."

"You hardly decimated me. You barely won," I point out.

"Stop flirting over there, and get in the car," Ashton calls back to us with a grin.

"We're not flirting," I say.

But then Jenni gives me a look like she wants me to be quiet.

Oh yeah. We're supposed to be pretending to be together.

"I mean..." I put my arm around her. "It's just a lover's quarrel."

"Lovers?" Mom says, walking back toward us. "Then it's true. When I went over to ask earlier, Meera said you were dating now, but I didn't believe her."

So Jenni had already told her mom... She should have communicated that to me because I feel like a fool. "That's right, Mom. Jenni is my girlfriend."

"And you're just now telling me this?"

Jenni is warm against my side. She feels nice there, like she fits into me. For a moment, it's almost like the rivalry is gone between us. But who am I kidding? She's only acting.

"I didn't know we were telling people yet." I look down at Jenni.

"We talked about it, babe."

Babe? Now we're using pet names? I'm so out of my league here.

"So that's why you took her on such a nice date!" Mom looks like a kid who just got a coveted toy on Christmas morning.

I can't help but feel a little guilty at the look of pure joy in my mom's eyes.

"That's right," Jenni says. "I couldn't help but fall for him after that." She snuggles into me.

She's good at this. I can barely tell she's acting, and it's taking my breath away to have her so close.

"Look at the two of you together!" Mom is ecstatic, and guilt creeps up at the web of lies we're spinning. Jenni and I haven't really talked through the logistics of how we're going to end this thing. I don't like the idea of toying with my mom's emotions. "Why don't the two of you come over for dinner tonight?"

That means we're going to have to continue this little act of ours. "Sure, Mom. What time?"

"Six o'clock."

Jenni smiles and looks up at me with an adoring look. "We'll be there."

I know none of this is real, but it's strange to see Jenni looking at me like that, and I'm not sure I know how I feel about it.

~

"Your relationship with Jenni had better be the fake one you were talking about."

Ronnie storms into the barn where I'm rewarding Thunder with an apple for a job well done. He may not have won, but he came in second place, which is still impressive.

"Keep your voice down," I say, glancing around to see who might have overheard us. When I don't see anyone, I'm able to breathe a bit easier.

"You don't have the best track record for being loyal, so excuse me if I'm a little concerned about my sister's heart getting broken."

"Ronnie, that was a long time ago. How many times do I have to tell you I'm sorry?" Maybe he's still hung up on Amanda.

He rubs the back of his neck and grimaces. "Once my trust is broken, it's hard to win it back."

"I'm well aware of that." I tug down on the cowboy hat I'm wearing. I've had it for a lot of years, and it's in surprisingly good condition. I have a large collection of cowboy hats, but I usually wear this one because it's my favorite. It's just stood the test of time.

"You and Jenni looked a little too cozy after the race."

"I told you it's fake. Jenni still can't stand me, if you want to know."

Ronnie leans against one of the stalls. "I'm not sure that's actually true."

My heart does a little flip flop in my chest at his words. "Why do you say that?" I keep my voice neutral, but my pulse has picked up.

"I think she's had a thing for you for a long time. And vice versa."

"What?" I scoff. "Hardly. She barely tolerates me."

Ronnie narrows his eyes. "But you two have chemistry, and I don't like it. Never have."

"Because you think I'll hurt her?"

Ronnie crosses his arms. "Look, if you could betray me like that, what's keeping you from betraying her too?"

"I would never hurt Jenni."

His voice grows menacing. "You'd better not."

It's nice to see that he wants to protect his sister, but does he have to turn that protectiveness onto me?

"There's nothing going on between us, so you have nothing to worry about."

Ronnie's shoulders relax a bit, but not completely. "And if there is, you'll have to answer to me."

~

When I get to my parents' historical home, Jenni is already there in the living room, playing the piano. She's very talented. I don't have a musical bone in my body, but I can appreciate it like the best of them.

Mittens and Zebra, the two gray striped cats that my parents have, chase each other across the living room, tumbling into one of their famous wrestling matches that they've been doing since they were kittens. Mittens swipes Zebra across the nose, and Zeb howls in pain.

"You two are worse than kids. No respect for Jenni's piano performance."

When Jenni finishes the song she's playing, she looks up at me. "Hey, babe." She gets up and walks up to me, slinging her arms around my shoulders. I try not to stiffen. It's so strange having her touch me like this, but it's nice too, which puts me on treacherous ground. I can't enjoy this too much.

"Wes," my mom calls to my father. "Look at how

adorable they are together." She claps her hands giddily.

Dad looks at us from over the book he's reading in his favorite chair by the fireplace. "I see that." He sets the book down and uncrosses his legs. "Is dinner ready yet?"

"I'll go check with Lidia." She heads toward the kitchen.

Jenni and I settle on the love seat across from my dad, and Mittens jumps up to curl up in my lap. "Sausage is going to smell you on me, and it's going to make him terribly jealous."

Zebra rubs against Jenni's legs. "Noodle will be jealous too, but he'll pretend he doesn't care."

Dad smiles at us. "Noodle and Sausage. It sounds like they go together. Maybe it's a sign."

I don't want to think about that. And from the look on Jenni's face, I can tell she doesn't either. But then she catches herself and flashes a big smile.

"Oh, Babe! Your dad is so right. It's definitely a sign."

Dad eyes the warmth between us. It may be fake, but even I'm starting to buy it. "I'm surprised you two are still dating after Valentine won the race today."

"I never said I was happy about it." Which is true.

Jenni only smiles and elbows me playfully. "He forgives me though."

Do I though?

"He might be a little bit of a sore loser, but our love is strong enough to withstand a little bit of jealousy, isn't it, Babe?"

She really wants to twist that knife, doesn't she?

I force a smile that I'm not feeling. "It sure is," I say through clenched teeth. She's going to pay for this later. How? I'm not sure yet, but I'll think of something.

Lidia comes in. "Dinner is ready."

Dad stands eagerly, setting his book on the table beside him. "Good. I'm starving."

The dining room still has the original woodwork from the 1800s, with the same table that's been there all along. Much of the furniture is original to the home and has been restored. The home has been in the Keith family for years and has been passed down from generation to generation.

Jenni takes a seat beside me, and my parents settle in their usual seats with my dad at the head of the table and my mother sitting beside him. My parents have a solid marriage with the kind of love story I'd like to have for myself one day. They're united and have withstood the stresses of running a worldwide commercial real estate corporation after all these years.

My father offers a blessing on the food, which looks to be roasted chicken with mashed potatoes and a variety of vegetables.

After the prayer, we dig into the food.

"Just think of all these years we've had Jenni over to share our dinner with us. I always hoped for a day that she would end up with one of my boys, and here we are." My mom's eyes glisten, and she wipes a tear away.

Great. Now my mom's crying, and I feel terrible for lying to her. I lean over to Jenni to whisper in her ear. But with her this close to me, I can smell the lavender shampoo she's using, and it's doing funny things to my insides. "Maybe this is a mistake."

She looks up at me and whispers back, "It's a little too late for that now. We're in this thing."

"Look at the two of them whispering sweet nothings to each other," my mom coos to my dad. "Next stop, marriage, and a whole slew of babies."

Jenni stiffens at her words. It's slight, but I don't miss it. Am I that repulsive to her?

"Maybe we shouldn't get ahead of ourselves," she says.

"Oh, don't mind me. You two take all the time you need. Relationships take time to blossom and grow."

Surely, she doesn't really mean that...

"But not too long." She grins at us both like she thinks her own joke is hilarious.

That's more like it. The mom I know and love, always pushing people to find lifelong romance.

Jenni takes my hand and squeezes it above the table so my parents can see. "I don't know how long we'll be able to wait. So don't you worry about that."

She's really laying it on thick here. I force a smile. "Isn't she the sweetest?" I fight off the temptation to elbow her to cool her jets.

If the goal here is to convince my parents to root for her instead of Amanda, she's done a spectacular job. She's due to show up tomorrow, and my heart pounds just thinking about it.

But I still don't know how they'll act when Amanda shows up. I hope we can keep up this ruse long enough to chase her off. After that, I'm putting an end to this nonsense. I only hope Jenni will allow it to end.

The next people we need to convince are her parents, and we might have to keep our fake relationship afloat long enough for her mom to give up on the idea that Jenni needs to be set up with a guy from India. And who knows how long that will take? We could be at this for years.

Would it be possible to pretend to date Jenni long term without letting my heart get involved?

7

JENNI

I pour myself a cup of peppermint tea and take it to my laptop in my office. It's getting late, but after Laurie's remark about Langston and me having a whole slew of babies, I can't stop thinking about fostering children. I settle into my desk chair and take a sip of tea as I open my browser. I search "How to become a foster parent in Georgia" and click on the top result.

I continue to sip my tea as I read through the information, my pulse quickening. Am I really ready to take such a huge step? There's a form I can fill out to get someone to contact me and discuss the process further. I hold my breath and then go for it. What can it hurt? I can at least get the ball rolling. If I decide later I'm not ready, then I can back out. But I see the faces of the children on the website, and it tugs on my heartstrings. These kids need help, and I can give them a good life. The best of the best. I could take them from hell to heaven. The thought warms me. Or maybe it's just the tea I just swallowed. Either way, I'm warm inside.

What if they give me a newborn? Like one dropped off at a fire station or something? I'd have to go out and buy everything for the little one. I don't even know everything a baby needs.

And what will I tell my mom? Because once a little one shows up at my house, there's no hiding the fact that I can't get pregnant.

But maybe I don't have to tell them I can't get pregnant. Couldn't I just say I want to help these kids and keep my fertility out of it?

I lean back in my desk chair and cross my ankles. That could actually work.

My house is so quiet. All I can hear at the moment is the occasional car driving down my street. My next-door neighbors have kids, and I hear them from time to time. If I got older kids, they'd have built-in friends next door.

I long to have my home filled with the noises children make. I have the dream job and all the money and success I could ever want. I'll end up being the vice president of my family's company one day. But the simplest thing, having kids, is impossible for me. It's heartbreaking on so many levels.

It doesn't help that Mom and Laurie sit around talking about how they want grandbabies all the time. I don't know if they'd accept my foster kids as grand-children, but I hope it will heal some of the heartache for them.

I take a deep breath, fill out the form, and hit submit.

~

The next morning before work, I head over to the stables on my parents' property to ride Marshmallow. I've already called over there ahead of time, so they'll have him ready for me when I get there. My boots tap across the pavement as I walk from my car to the stable. The air is crisp, but not too cool. Just refreshingly so. I see Langston riding Thunder off in the distance, and he must have spotted me because now he's riding in my direction. Since his land is connected to my parents' land, he comes over this way often when he rides.

I head into the barn, and Marshmallow is already saddled up and ready to go. Langston dismounts and walks toward me before I have a chance to get up in the saddle. He looks good in a cowboy hat, plaid shirt, and jeans. I can't see his rear from here, but I get the impression that it isn't too bad looking in those jeans he's wearing. I've seen him in jeans many times before, and let's just say that they fit him well and leave it at that...

"Hey, my love," I say in a flirtatious tone.

His eyebrows raise. "Love? I didn't know we were taking our relationship to the next level already."

I roll my eyes. Can't he just play along? I force a smile, fighting to keep my frustration out of it. The people who watch over the horses here are probably still hanging around, and I know they talk amongst themselves. News would travel lightning fast if they caught wind that we were putting on an act for our parents.

And I can't have that.

"You getting in a ride before work?" I ask.

"Sure looks that way, doesn't it?"

"When is Amanda getting into town?" I lean against the stall door.

"Sometime tonight."

He smells nice, like he's wearing woodsy cologne.

"Are you nervous?"

"You want the truth?" He licks his lips, and I can't ignore the way the motion catches my attention. His lips are full and soft-looking. My heart pounds to think that he might be kissing me with those lips sometime soon, which is crazy. This is Langston, the pain in my rear and biggest rival.

I nod, taking my gaze up to his baby blue eyes.

Langston has always been the best looking of all the Keith boys. He's got those broad shoulders and a perfectly trimmed beard. Sometimes it's just a light covering of scruff, which is also flattering on him.

"The truth is, I'm terrified of seeing her again."

I'm not sure how I feel about that. It shouldn't matter, but part of me is worried he still has it bad for her. And I don't like it one bit. "Why are you terrified?" I don't really want to know the answer, but my mouth betrays me and the words spill out anyway.

"I don't know what she's going to say."

"Are you worried she's going to want to get back together with you?" I can't help but ask it because that's really my main concern, which is stupid. Langston and I aren't really anything more than friends, and barely at that.

I was just thinking about how kissable his lips might be, but that's beside the point.

"I don't know what I feel. I just know that my heart pounds thinking about what she's going to say." His mouth is turned downward.

"So your heart is pounding like she's a special someone, or it's pounding because you're anxious?" Do I really want to know the answer?

"I'm anxious. It feels like she has something she's going to hold over my head, and I don't know what it is." His eyebrows knit together.

He's upset about this. And there's this twinge inside my heart I don't usually have for him. I feel bad for him. For whatever reason, I don't want to see Langston worked up about her. "I'm sorry," I whisper. "I have no idea what this must be like for you."

He shrugs. "I'll find out soon enough what the truth is."

"I thought you were convinced she was a gold digger."

"I'm not ruling that out, but I can't help this nagging feeling that something else is going on. Something bigger."

I scrunch my brow. "What gives you that idea?"

"It's subtle. Nothing she says. It's just the tone of her voice or something. I can't put my finger on it."

"Did she call you?"

"Yeah. Just briefly to make arrangements of where she'd stay and for how long."

"What's the plan then?"

"She's going to meet us at my parents' home and will be staying with them for a week."

"So long?"

"Yeah. She wouldn't say why though."

I reach out and put a hand on his arm. "I hope everything goes well for you tonight."

He lets out a sigh. "Me too."

"Do you want me to be there?"

"It would probably be a good idea if we're doing this whole ... um, relationship thing." I can tell he was about to say "fake relationship" but stopped himself so no one would overhear.

"Of course. We need to show Amanda right off the bat that we're together and madly in love."

I drop my hand from his arm. "Oh, so now you agree to being in love?"

He laughs and shushes me. "Of course." He lowers his voice and leans toward me. "And keep your voice down. I just saw someone walking around a minute ago. The last thing we need is for someone to overhear what we're saying."

He's standing so close to me, near enough that I can see a ring of green around his pupil. His eyes are even more beautiful up close.

The next thing I know, I'm being nudged from behind, and I fall into Langston's arms. "Oof." What was that?

Langston encircles me into his embrace as he steadies me. "Marshmallow, what was that for?"

I turn to see Marshmallow innocently munching on hay. "Was that him?"

"I saw him do it. He pushed you right into my arms."

I step back from Langston and can't help but laugh. "That crazy horse."

But once again, Marshmallow nudges me in the back, into Langston's arms again. This time Langston's more prepared. I look up into his eyes, and my breath catches. His arms are warm and strong around me. We're frozen like this for a moment, and time stands still. My gaze trails down to his lips where they linger. What would it be like to kiss him? I can't help but wonder. Is he good at it? There's no way this guy is a terrible kisser. I don't get that vibe from him. But how can I really know without trying it out?

Langston's watching me, and he leans down. The moment before his lips touch mine, Raul, the stable manager, comes around the corner.

"Oh, I didn't mean to interrupt you two."

I pull away from Langston, heat creeping across my cheeks. My breath is coming out ragged and short, and I turn and steady my gaze onto Marshmallow. Raul has the worst timing out of anyone on the planet.

"Your horse is quite the matchmaker," Langston says to me, his voice low and husky.

It sends a chill down my spine to hear him speak to me so intimately, like it's our little secret.

I step away from him and shake off the haze that seems to have settled itself comfortably in my brain. "Marshmallow, you troublemaker."

Langston pulls me toward him with Raul in plain view. "He doesn't seem like he's causing trouble to me."

Langston is putting on a show, right? None of this is

real. It's almost like I imagined the fact that he almost kissed me. I play along with the act and put my head on his shoulder and pretend not to notice how muscled and hard it is. "Should we get going with our morning ride? I have to get to work in about an hour."

"Of course. Let's get going."

I open Marshmallow's stall and lead him out so I can have some room to mount him. I often ride in the mornings, as does Langston, but we haven't really ridden together like this before.

We take the trail that leads back to his property, talking about work and some of the drama with other employees treating him badly because he's the boss's son.

"I know the feeling well." I twist the reins in my hands as we head down the trail, side by side. "I've had to work much harder than those around me to prove that I'm not just winning favors from my dad. It doesn't help that I'm a girl either. People always assume I'm a little behind the curve because of it. There are a lot of arrogant men in this industry."

"Kaison told me Ariana has dealt with that a lot too. Maybe you could talk to her about it sometime," Langston suggests.

"Oh, we've talked about it plenty. Believe me. She's told me all about how when she was first hired at Keith Enterprises to revamp the entire department, some jerk wanted to put her office in a closet instead of a regular office." Just because she's a woman. It's even worse in some ways being the owner's daughter. A lot of people in the office resent me for it and assume I'm just a spoiled princess with everything handed to me.

"I heard Kaison ended up giving her the jerk's office." A branch brushes against Langston's shoulder.

"And then they ended up together. Sounds like that decision paid off for him."

Another branch comes along and knocks his hat right off his head.

"I think you're missing something there," I say.

Langston reaches up to pat his bare head and then twists to look behind him where his hat is floating in a mud puddle. "Shoot. That's my favorite hat, and now it's going to be all muddy."

I slow Marshmallow to a stop and climb down to the ground. The mud, still wet from the downpour that lasted most of the night, squishes below my cowgirl boots. The bad thing about these boots is that they have no tread and tend to be slippery. So I walk gingerly over to where the hat is floating around like a boat in the mud puddle.

Langston's steps suck into the mud as he comes up behind me.

"You didn't have to get down," I say. "I've got it covered."

"It's my fault that I wasn't watching for the

branches better, so I should be the one down in the mud. Not you."

"Langston Keith? Are you actually being nice to me?" I look around. "No one's even here to witness this."

He trudges through the muck as he catches up beside me. "I can be nice. In fact, most people would say I'm a great guy."

I give him the side eye. "You probably haven't thrown those people into a lake when it's forty-seven degrees out."

He throws his head back and laughs. "That was a good day, wasn't it?"

"Maybe once I had my dry clothes back on."

Langston's face goes weird, and then his cheeks get all red.

Wait a second... "Were you picturing me naked just now?"

His mouth forms an *O* like he'd just been caught.

"You'd better clean up your mind. Because we're just friends, remember?"

His spine stiffens. "Thank you for making that perfectly clear. But I remember. You won't have to worry about that."

I've made him angry. But I refuse to feel bad about it. I stomp away from him toward the fallen hat. I reach down to get it, but it's floating to the middle of this huge puddle and I can't reach it. Maybe if I just stretch a bit more, I can get it.

But now I'm starting to lose my balance, and my slippery shoes slide across the mud. I wave my arms around like an angry goose, trying to keep from falling into the puddle. Langston steps to catch me, but it's too late. Just as his arms reach around my waist, I fall face first into the mini lake. The water splashes around me as I hit the ground. And I've brought Langston down with me. He must have lost his footing as I tipped forward. We're in a heap of arms and legs, all tangled up in the mud. And it's everywhere. All in my hair, up my nose, and some has even gotten in my mouth. I crawl from under Langston, and he scoots through the mud away from me before standing.

I get on my hands and knees, my hair dripping, and stand, spitting the mud out of my mouth onto the ground beside me.

The hat is still floating in the puddle like we haven't even been there.

Langston must have spotted it too because he swoops down to get it, and he crams it onto his head. Water drips down his cheeks and over his ears.

I can't help but laugh. There's nothing else we can do in this situation. "Why'd you put your hat on?"

"I figured I'm already covered in mud. What's it matter now? I might as well enjoy my favorite hat."

"It's a good look on you." I snicker.

"Oh, you like it?" Langston gives me a crooked grin. "You should see yourself. You look like you went to one of those mud spas they have at those fancy resorts my dad owns."

I wipe the mud from my nose, which only smears more across my face. I don't feel like getting my saddle muddy, so I grab Marshmallow and walk with him back to the stable, with Langston doing the same with Thunder.

"I'm going to need five showers after this."

"I think I'll take one really long one," Langston responds.

I nod. "That would probably work just as well."

"Do you think people will assume we were out here doing more than riding horses?"

"Well, we are a couple, but that would be weird."

I can't help but dissolve into giggles.

"What's so funny?"

"Romance in the mud? How did I even think of this?"

"I don't know, but it doesn't sound like fun."

"I know!" I say. "It's because I have a dirty mind! Get it? Dirty mind?"

"You're hilarious," Langston says in a flat voice.

"Oh, come on. You thought it was funny, admit it."

"I guess it would be funny if you're into dad jokes."

"You're nothing but a big old grump." I bend down

and scoop up a handful of soggy mud and fling it at him. It lands square in the middle of his back.

"Oh, no you didn't!" Langston spins around, bends down to get his own scoop of mud, and I quickly duck to get my own. I'm sensing that I just started World War III.

But as I'm reaching down to get more ammo, Langston's shot hits me right on the crown of my head, mud splattering everywhere.

"That was loud." I lob another shot at him, and this time, I hit him in the shoulder.

"You're asking for it."

And bedlam breaks out, each of us scooping up handfuls of mud and tossing it at the other as quickly as possible. The horses are covered, we're covered, and the trees around us are covered.

Marshmallow backs away from us, not that I blame him, and I allow it. He didn't ask to be a part of our war zone. I reach down to grab my next handful, but there's something different about this pile of mud. It's warm. Before I can think too hard about what that might mean, it's out of my hand and splatting into Langston's cheek.

It registers just as his eyes go wide. "Did you just throw manure at me?"

"I—uh... I didn't know it was manure. I thought it was just mud." But there's a stench on my hands.

"You've taken it too far this time." Langston charges, and we both hit the mud with a loud splat.

Langston is on top of me, mud dripping from his face to mine. How romantic.

"You're cutting off my air supply."

He laughs and rolls off of me. "Truce?"

"Fine. Truce."

I get back to Marshmallow, who seems to have calmed down now that we've ceased fire.

"I'm not looking forward to the walk back." Oh shoot. "How am I going to get in my car like this?"

"Don't worry. I'll hose you down," Langston offers.

"Or we could just go jump in the lake again," I say.

"I'll pass. I'm not in the mood for that icy water again."

"I thought you were all tough. What happened?"

"Once every year or two is enough for me."

I laugh as we head back to the stables. My parents are sitting on their back patio when we get there. They like to eat breakfast out there sometimes.

"What happened to you two?" my mom calls to us.

"We fell in the mud, Mom. And then we might have gotten into a mud fight..."

"Ahh, young love. It's a little strange, but whatever." She gives me a wide grin. "As long as you two get married and give me lots of grandbabies, I'll accept it."

My chest gets tight at her words, but I try not to show it. I know she's trying to make a joke, but I'm not laughing. "Langston and I just got together. You don't want us rushing things, do you?"

She waves a hand dismissively. "I don't see why it needs to take a long time. When you know. You know."

But we need this to take a super long time. Otherwise, she'll just go back to setting me up with some guy in India I've never met.

And I can't have that.

8

LANGSTON

"Let's go hose each other off," Jenni tells me after her mom goes back into the house.

"I'm not sure I trust you with a hose pointed at me," I say.

"So you're just going to walk home like that, dripping across your floors?" Jenni asks.

I hadn't thought this far ahead. "Fine. You're right."

"I'm right?" She gets this huge smile on her face. "Can you say that again?"

"Why?" I arch a brow at her.

"Because I want to bask in this moment."

"Oh, brother." I roll my eyes. "Let's just get the water hose."

Luckily, there's a warm water option on the hoses, since the horses need warm water in the winter.

I stand outside the stable and Jenni drags the hose over to where I am, spraying me down.

I scream like a little girl. "I thought you were going to use warm water!"

"Where would be the fun in that?" Jenni gives me an evil grin.

"This is just wrong." I stalk past her and adjust the water to a warmer setting. "That was inhumane."

She's bent over laughing. "You should have heard yourself," she says between giggles.

I walk over to where she's still holding the hose and put my hand in the stream. "That's much better."

"You know you started this." Jenni grins mockingly at me.

"How is it my fault that you just sprayed me down with ice cold water when you could have used warm water?"

"You're the one who put the idea in my head when you said you didn't trust me with the hose." She points the hose to me, and the water forcefully hits my chest, splattering mud up into my face. I squeeze my eyes and mouth shut as she moves from my chest to my arms. I turn around so she can get my back. Then I peel my shirt off because it's grown heavy and is sticking to my torso.

Jenni is staring at me.

"Were you just checking me out?" I grin.

Her cheeks go red. "No..."

"Sure seems like you were."

"Where else am I supposed to look? I'm spraying you down."

"But do you have to look at me like that?"

"Like what?" She moves the spray to my legs, and the mud runs down me in rivers. "This is just how my face looks."

"You know, it's okay if you want to check me out. You don't have to feel ashamed of your feelings for me."

Jenni narrows her eyes at me and angles the hose at my face.

I block the spray with my hands and dance away as she chases me with it.

I may be teasing her about checking me out, but the truth is, I felt something strong between us earlier when we almost kissed. And I want to explore whatever that might be.

It's a terrible idea, though, because I don't want to face Ronnie's wrath. I value my life too much to go there with Jenni. I just need to keep it together better, which means I can't allow us to be in that situation again. It's easier said than done with us constantly in romantic situations.

And I may have been teasing her about checking me out, but the truth is I can hardly keep my eyes off of her either, even fully clothed and covered in mud.

"You want me to spray you down?" I offer when I'm done with my turn.

"Nope." She turns the stream of water onto herself, mud traveling down her in tiny rivers.

"Why not? You're not going to be able to get the back of you very well."

"I can angle it like this and get it clean just fine." She puts the sprayer above her head and points it to go over her like a shower.

"Isn't that hurting your arms?" I ask.

"Not a bit."

But it will pretty soon. "How are you going to get all that mud out of your hair without my help? You're not scared to let me do it, are you?"

"I wouldn't use the word scared. More like smart. I'm too smart to let you spray me down," she clarifies.

I grin. "Are you saying you don't trust me?"

"Yes." She smiles back at me as she sprays down her hair. "That's exactly what I'm saying."

"What if I promise to not spray you in the face?" The wind hits me, and I shiver. I could really use a real shower and a change of clothes.

She sprays down her arms. "No need. I'm almost done."

One of the Finley household staff members approaches us with an armful of towels. "Jenni, your mother sent me out here to bring you two some towels.

She said you're both welcome to dry off and use her showers to get cleaned up."

Jenni turns to me. "How are we always getting ourselves into these situations?"

I laugh. "I couldn't tell you."

~

*M*y assistant, Maggie, brought over a change of clothes for me while I was in the shower. I ended up being late to work, but since I work from home, it's not like anyone was there to get me in trouble, though I try to stay on a regular schedule to increase my productivity.

During my afternoon meeting, I struggle to focus on the discussion about the merger in Singapore, instead finding my thoughts straying to Amanda's arrival later today and the almost-kiss between Jenni and me.

By five p.m., I'm exhausted, even though it was a relatively easy day. Since I got started late, normally I would end up working later, but Amanda is due to arrive at Mom and Dad's house by six, and I want to be there when she arrives.

I head straight over there as soon as I'm done with work.

"Amanda's not here yet," Mom says after I've arrived. She's knitting in her favorite chair in the upstairs sitting area. It used to be a bedroom, but she turned it into her craft room. Half the room is full of various yarns, and the other half is a place for her to sit and knit with room for her friends to join her as well. "But Jenni just texted. She's on her way right now. Are you sure you want Jenni here when Amanda arrives?"

"Jenni's my girlfriend. There's nothing Amanda can say that I wouldn't want her to hear."

"I know. But your relationship is still new, and I'd hate to have Amanda ruin things between you." Mom continues knitting.

"I'm not worried about it. Jenni and I are rock solid," I lie. Well, maybe it isn't quite a lie. Our *fake* relationship is rock solid. Because Jenni wants the protection I can offer from her mom's scheming.

Mom looks over at the east-facing windows. "Speaking of, it looks like she's pulling up right now."

I glance down and see her red sports car parked in the front drive from my second story view. "I'm going to go talk to her."

"You go see your sweetheart. I'll just be up here, watching for Amanda to arrive." Her knitting needles click together as she speaks.

I head downstairs to see the butler, Gregory, opening the door for Jenni. My parents keep a full staff, just like our ancestors have for many years. They're old fashioned like that, and they're proud to provide the jobs for their household.

"Hey." I rush toward her across the white marble floor and take her into my arms, aware of Gregory's eyes on us. She feels amazing in my arms as her body melts against mine like she's always belonged there.

She pulls away from me. "You're acting like you haven't seen me in days." She smiles at me with love in her eyes. It pummels me in the gut, and I have to remind myself it's not real.

"It's been too long," I say, laying it on thick. "I can't stand to be away from you."

Gregory doesn't comment, which is typical for him. He's not exactly the warm, fuzzy type. He takes his job very seriously and is strictly professional around the family.

Jenni and I head into the living room together and settle on the couch next to the grand piano. Tall windows overlook the backyard and the stables beyond.

"You ready to see Amanda?" Jenni asks. She takes my hand in hers and it's warm, soft, and small in mine. Most of the time Jenni seems strong and impenetrable, but seeing how small her hand is in mine gives me a protective feeling that I'm not used to having toward her.

"Honestly? No."

Jenni's expression is soft, and I get the impression that she's not faking it this time. She squeezes my hand. "Everything will work out."

"What can she possibly have to say that's so important that she has to come all this way to tell me in person?" I breathe in Jenni's lavender shampoo, and it's comforting.

"Either she wants money, or she's interested in getting back together."

"Maybe she wants a job." The idea just popped into my head and it's something I haven't considered before.

"It would be smart for her to come out here to your parents' house to work her way into your family's hearts," Jenni says.

Would it be though? "I'm not sure I'd want to hire her based on that. And wouldn't she have said something about wanting to be hired over the phone if that were the case?" She really has me stumped.

"Maybe we should talk about something else to get your mind off of this until she comes." Jenni looks up into my eyes, and they're full of tenderness that I'm not used to seeing. She's beautiful this way. Soft instead of her normal hard exterior.

"What did you have in mind?"

She traces her fingers down the bare skin of my lower arm. I have my shirt sleeves rolled up because it's gotten warmer as the day has gone on.

"What's your favorite childhood memory?"

I have to think about that. "When it snowed here back when I was ten. We all went sledding together and had this giant snowball fight with snow forts and everything, and then we came inside and had cookies and hot chocolate."

Jenni's face lit up with a big smile. "I remember that. I made snow angels."

I can't help smiling back at her. "We didn't get as many snow days as I would have liked as a kid."

"No we didn't. We had to rely on trips to Utah for snow skiing to see the real snow."

My parents love snow skiing and have a house in Park City that we like to visit every winter. They keep properties all over the world. We're big on traveling in the Keith family.

"I'm absolutely terrible at skiing," Jenni moans.

"Remember the time you tried taking that jump?"

"Don't remind me of that. It ended quite tragically. My tailbone still hurts just thinking about that."

"What made you do it to begin with? I just remember seeing you flying through the air and crashing. It looked brutal."

"I thought I was being adventurous." Jenni giggles. "I was never dumb enough to try that again." She looks over at me with a crooked grin. "In the meantime, you're whizzing down the black diamonds."

"I'd say some of those ski slopes in Utah are even better than the skiing in the Swiss Alps."

"Oh, but you can't beat the adventure of going to Europe." Jenni gets this wistful look in her eyes.

"Or India." I've been there many times with her family over the years.

"India is the best. But of course I'm biased. I love the culture and seeing my mom's family. It's just good to revisit your roots, you know?"

"Then why didn't you want to date a guy from India?"

"It doesn't have anything to do with the fact that he's from India. That I have no problem with. I just don't want to be set up with someone I don't pick out myself."

"Have you ever thought about dating a guy from India?"

"Sure. Plenty of times. I've even talked to a bunch of Indian guys online." She makes a face. "I don't recommend using dating apps. You meet a lot of creepers that way."

"But wouldn't you be more likely to find a decent guy if you're taking recommendations from your aunts?"

"Hey, my mom didn't have to do the arranged marriage thing. I don't think I should have to either."

"It is kind of ironic that she was pushing you to try an arranged marriage."

"I don't know that she was going to take it that far, but she was inching into that territory." Jenni runs her fingers through her jet-black hair. It looks touchable and soft.

I reach out to feel it, stroking my fingers through it. I half expect her to stiffen up at my touch, but she doesn't. If anything, she looks relaxed, like she's enjoying it. But I can't tell if she's putting on an act for the staff members passing by or if she really likes it.

"Well, don't you two look cozy." I look up to see Mom coming downstairs. "Amanda just pulled up."

My heart starts to pound at her words.

"Just take a deep breath, Langston." Jenni takes my hand and interlocks her fingers with mine supportively. "Everything will be okay."

Her eyes are sincere, and I know for a fact she's not acting. She's actually being really sweet. It's a side of Jenni I've rarely seen. Usually, she's wearing this prickly exterior. I wouldn't ever have called her tender before, but that's what she's like at the moment.

The doorbell sounds, and Gregory's footsteps hitting the marble ring through the house as he goes to let her in.

I stand because I don't know what else to do. It's dumb. I shouldn't care this much about what Amanda wants. It's not like I have any feelings for her. Those have long evaporated.

Her voice drifts in from the foyer, talking to Gregory in a tone too low to understand.

When Gregory appears on the other side of the wall with the giant fireplace, he has Amanda with him as well as a boy who appears to be about seven or eight.

I was expecting Amanda to look vibrant and full of life, like she's hunting for a man, but this woman looks emaciated and pale, like she's been malnourished. She has dark bags under her eyes, and they're sunken into her face with her cheekbones sticking out. Her hair is different too. It's short, choppy, and thin. Far from the luscious long hair she had when I last saw her. Has she been starving herself or something?

But the kid with her is the picture of health. He has thick dark hair and eyes that are roaming across the room like he's never seen a place like this before. The home is like a museum, similar to Biltmore, where they charge admission to get inside.

"Hi, I'm Langston. What's your name?" I shake the little boy's hand and look into eyes that mirror my own.

"I'm Hayden." He smiles at me, and two dimples pop, one on each cheek, just like the ones I have.

"Langston," Amanda says, stepping toward me. And as she gets closer, she looks even more frail than I'd originally thought. Her movements are slow, like they're taking a lot out of her. "It's been a long time."

"Should we go sit down?" Mom asks, gesturing to the living room.

We shuffle to the couches and settle around the blazing fireplace.

Amanda looks uncomfortable in her own skin, like she doesn't know what to say.

Why would she come here with a child? My chest turns to stone, and I can't breathe. The room starts to spin around me.

It's been nine years since I've seen her last. Is it possible that this kid could be mine? That could be why she darted off so quickly without an explanation. "How can I help you?" It's clear she's in a bad way. If she's come here to take advantage of me, she's doing an excellent job of it.

"How old are you?"

"I'm eight."

"I remember being eight," I say stupidly. Because all I can think is, what if this kid is mine...

"Hayden"—I put an arm around Jenni's shoulders —"this is my girlfriend, Jenni."

Surprise flits across Amanda's sunken features. "Are you two dating now?"

"Yes, it's new, but things are going well," Jenni says.

"I'm happy for you both." She sounds genuine, which is a relief.

Mom looks to Amanda, then to me, and finally to Hayden. When she looks back at me, she raises her eyebrows. "Do you think..." She gestures to Hayden but then presses her lips together. "We're glad to have you come stay with us," she says to Hayden.

"Amanda, you still haven't told us why you've come all this way," I begin.

She looks at the people surrounding us. "Would it be okay if we spoke privately, Langston?"

"Of course," I say. "We can go to the conference room." I get up, and I follow her in that direction. She's been to my parents' place many times, so she's familiar with the house.

When we get to the conference room, I shut the door, and we sit at the table.

"I'm sorry to spring this on you," she says, twisting her hands in her lap.

"I still don't understand why you couldn't just call me instead of coming all this way." My pulse is racing.

"I wanted you to meet Hayden."

"Okay... Is there something you need to tell me about him?" I rub my sweaty palms together.

"I have stage four breast cancer, and I've been given six months to live," she blurts, raising her gaze to mine, completely ignoring my question.

You could hear a pin drop in the room. It's not what I was expecting her to say, but given her frail appearance, it makes sense now. "I'm sorry to hear that," I finally respond.

"It's been a tough road." Amanda sighs. "Hayden has been so strong through all of this."

"That's hard, but it still doesn't explain why you're here." My chest hurts from anxiety.

"I was hoping you could help me..." Amanda trails off, looking down at her hands.

Here it comes. She's looking for money, after all.

"Langston," Amanda says, meeting my eye. Her hands are fidgeting again. "I—I wasn't quite clear just now. Hayden is ... *our* son."

9

JENNI

*H*ayden is Langston's son. I knew it the minute those dimples showed up on that kid's face. He looks *exactly* like Langston. Same hair, same eyes, same smile, dimples and all. I'd still want a paternity test if I were Langston just to cover my bases, but the truth is right in front of our faces.

Does Hayden know? And is that what Amanda is telling him in there, that she's been hiding this kid from Langston for *eight* years?

If it were my child, I'd be livid.

I'm already furious for him. How could she have done this to him? Not only did she abandon him right after they got married, but then she realized she was pregnant and didn't bother to call? Or did she already know she was pregnant and then decided to leave?

"I'm hungry," Hayden says. "Do you guys have any snacks around here, Grandma?"

Laurie and I freeze and stare at each other. A huge smile spreads across her face, and I get the impression she really likes being called Grandma by this kid. Does he just assume we both know the truth?

Laurie recovers quicker than I do, acting as though it's nothing out of the ordinary for him to call her that. "Well, of course we do. We're about to have dinner, but I guess it wouldn't hurt to sneak in a little cookie before we eat. Let's go see what Lidia can get for you."

"Who is Lidia?" Hayden stands.

"She's our cook."

Hayden's eyes get big. "You have your own cook?"

"Yes, and she's the nicest lady you'll ever meet," I say, getting up with them, and we head down the hall toward the kitchen. My heart is pounding. Langston is a dad... How weird is that? It's a lot to take in all at once. And it's not even my kid.

That has to be what Amanda is telling him in there. She's got him cornered with the kid right in front of him, so he can't turn the child away. How messed up is it that she would do that? What if Langston was a jerk and made a scene? How damaging could that be to Hayden?

Mittens, one of the family cats, trots behind us as we pass the dining room on our way to the kitchen.

She purrs and rubs up against Hayden like he's one of us.

"Do you like animals, Hayden?" I ask.

"I love them," he says. "I want to be a vet when I grow up."

"Well, there are plenty of animals around here," Laurie says, her face brightening. "This little one is named Mittens."

Hayden smiles. "I like that name."

"We also have Zeb, short for Zebra. He's her brother," Laurie tells him.

Hayden scratches behind Mittens' ears, and she rubs her head into his hand, requesting more.

"And... Langston has a dog at his house too. A very fat one," I say. I almost said "your dad" but then I figured I'd be assuming too much.

"Hey, no body shaming. We wouldn't want Sausage getting self-esteem issues," Laurie says.

I laugh. "He's at Langston's house. It's not like he can hear us."

"It's the principle of the thing." Laurie crosses his arms.

"I like dogs too," Hayden says.

"Then you'll have to come over and meet him. He's a very friendly dog," I say.

Hayden smiles, but not big enough for his dimples to show. I can't help but wonder if he's nervous about going to his dad's house.

We head into the kitchen where Lidia is standing at the stove cooking ground beef.

"Would it be possible to get a cookie for this kiddo?" Laurie asks.

Lidia turns to look at him. "Who do we have here?"

"I'm Hayden."

Lidia gives Laurie a questioning look.

"Amanda's son," Laurie says.

Lidia studies the boy and raises her eyebrows but doesn't ask the question that is clearly on her lips. *Is this Langston's son?*

"It's nice to meet you, Hayden. Do you want a chocolate chip cookie or a sugar cookie?"

The woman is an angel for not questioning further.

"Chocolate chip, please."

"Oh, he has nice manners too." Lidia beams at him as she turns to the pantry.

She comes back with a container filled with fresh-baked cookies and opens it for Hayden to get one.

I look down at Hayden as he munches his cookie.

"Do you guys have any video games here?"

"We sure do," Laurie says. "Every game system you can think of. Board games too. There were a lot of boys who grew up here, and they all loved playing video games."

"Awesome!"

"I bet we still have a little bit of time before dinner starts if you want to play for a while," Laurie says. "I don't know much about video games, but I bet Jenni could show you everything."

Laurie and I lead him to the upstairs family room. Langston's family may not be big on technology, but they did let their sons have whatever gaming systems they wanted.

We head down the hall, and we lead him to the room with all the electronics.

"This is so cool." Hayden runs into the room and makes a beeline for the TV cabinet, rummaging around through the stacks of games there.

It does my heart good to see the joy on his face, and I suddenly want to show him everything there is to do here. Is this what it would be like to have a foster child? Obviously, it would be a lot harder to have the full responsibility of raising a kid on my shoulders, but this moment is giving me a glimpse of what it might be like for me.

We all have so much love to give him.

"Are you guys going to let me live here?" Hayden asks.

Laurie and I exchange a glance over his head. "Is that why you're here?"

"Yeah, my mom has cancer. She's too sick to take care of me, so she needs my dad to help out."

"Oh, your poor mom. I had no idea," Laurie says.

That would explain why she looked so pale and thin.

"And you know who your dad is?" Laurie is treading lightly, but I can tell from the look in her eyes that she's dying to get answers. Not that I can blame her. I'm in the same boat.

"Yeah. Of course. He's Langston."

I let out a breath I hadn't realized I'd been holding. So it really is true.

"But I don't know why you guys want me to call him by his first name. He's my dad."

I open my mouth to speak, but then I just shut it again.

"You can call him whatever name you'd like," Laurie says.

"Anything?" Hayden gets a silly grin on his face. "Even Mr. Stinky Pants?"

I can't help but laugh. "If you really want to."

"He's not nearly as stinky now as he used to be," Laurie says. "He earned the name Mr. Stinky Pants when he was a baby. You don't even want to know what he smelled like back then." She pinches her nose and waves a hand in front of her face like she's blowing the stench away.

That gets a bubble of laughter from Hayden. "My mom's friend has a baby. He sure smells bad too."

"I'm afraid we're all stinky from time to time," Laurie says.

"Even you, Grandma?"

Laurie looks like she's not sure whether she wants

to laugh at his question or cry at the fact that he's calling her grandma.

"Not her," I say. "She only smells like roses all the time."

Hayden laughs. "I think I like it here."

"I've raised five boys. I'm not afraid of a little potty humor," Laurie says.

Hayden looks over at me. "Are you going to marry my dad?"

My mouth falls open. That was the last question I expected him to ask. This just got a whole lot more complicated. I look over to Laurie for help, silently begging her to change the subject.

But then Lidia comes into the room. "Dinner is ready."

Hayden pops up from the couch, but then he looks back at the TV. "I didn't get to finish my game though."

"Don't worry, Hayden," Laurie says. "You can come right back up here after you're finished with your dinner. You won't regret it. Lidia's tacos will melt right in your mouth."

"Okay." He sets his controller down and gets up to follow us back downstairs. As we're walking down the hall, Hayden turns and looks up at me with a nervous look on his face. "Do you think my dad is going to like me? Sometimes I don't remember to hang my backpack up after school, and I leave my coat in the middle of the floor."

I stop and turn to look him in the eyes. "Hayden, it doesn't matter what you do. Your dad is going to love you with every fiber of his being."

"But how do you know?"

"Because your dad is one of the best people I've ever met." And as I say it, I know it's true. He's kind and selfless and funny.

Laurie is speechless for once. She's just looking at me over his head, and I realize she's holding back tears and doesn't want him to see. She has a hand covering her mouth like she's hoping to silence any cries that might escape.

Amanda and Langston are sitting at the table when we get down there.

I meet his eyes and take a seat next to him. His eyes are full of tenderness when he sees Hayden.

"Hey, buddy. I heard you were up playing video games. I'm sorry I didn't know who you were before, but your mom told me, and we're good now. But I did have a feeling about it." He twists toward Hayden, who is passing behind his chair to the other side of him. "You kind of look like me." He looks over at me and mouths, "Did you know?"

I nod and lean over and whisper in his ear. "Hayden told your mom and me."

"Can I sit by you, Dad?" Hayden stands behind the empty chair next to Langston.

Langston looks at Hayden like he's the most

precious creature on earth, and my heart is melting watching the two of them together. "Of course." Langston pats the chair on the other side of him.

Amanda is sitting across from us, watching the interchange with a neutral expression on her face. I still can't help but wonder why she kept Hayden away from us for so long.

Laurie sits at the head of the table where Langston's dad usually sits. He's been away on a business trip and probably doesn't know anything about his new grandson. Laurie hasn't had a moment to tell him. But I have no doubt that she'll be picking up the phone as soon as she can.

Langston is a natural with Hayden. The two of them are cracking jokes back and forth all through dinner, like estranged friends making up for lost time.

After dinner, Amanda, Langston, Laurie, and I go to sit in the living room. Lidia takes Hayden back upstairs to play video games.

Langston begins, "You've probably figured it out by now that Hayden is my son."

"Hayden told us," Laurie says.

"I'm sorry you had to find out that way," Amanda says. "I didn't know a better way to tell you without it being in front of him."

"It's okay," Laurie says. "We're just glad to meet him."

I want to ask why he's just now allowed to be in our

lives, but I figure it's not my place to ask. I'm just the fake girlfriend in this scenario. As much as I want to be a bigger part of Hayden's life, that's the truth of the matter.

"Amanda wants to start fifty-fifty custody," Langston says.

"I have cancer, and it's become too much for me to care for Hayden on my own. We'll start with fifty-fifty, but on my bad days, I might need you to take him more. I just know I can't be the mom that he needs.'"

"Do you have family who could help you through this?" I ask.

Amanda shakes her head. "They've all either stopped talking to me, or they've passed on. I have no one left. That's why I need your help."

From what I remember, Amanda's family was a lot of drama. Something about her dad abandoning them when they were little and her mom struggling with a drug addiction. As a result, a bunch of the kids ended up having a lot of emotional problems as adults. I can't help but wonder if her mom was one of the ones who'd passed on.

"I don't understand why you kept him from me all these years."

Amanda crosses her arms defensively and juts her jaw out like she's ready to take whatever he can dish. "You're welcome to be upset about it, but I can't change the past."

Laurie pats Langston on the knee. "She's right, honey. All we can do now is move forward. We're just glad that you've brought Hayden to us now."

Langston works his jaw, and it's clear he's holding back words he doesn't feel he can say.

"We need to do what's best for Hayden," I say, taking my spot back in the armchair. "Right now he's going to need some stability. He already has lots of things in his life changing beyond his control. Let's not overwhelm him with too much attention. He has four uncles, an aunt, an almost aunt, two grandparents, friends in town, and loving staff members. Everyone will want to know him. Not to mention kids at his new school. All of a sudden there will be a new Keith in Blue Mountain. You don't think the town will want to get to know him?"

"I hadn't even thought about all that." Laurie sits back on the couch with a pensive look on her face.

"I've thought about it a little," Amanda says. "I think we start with him getting to know the people in this household. Then he can move on to Langston's house and stay there during the day. When school starts back up after spring break, I'd like to begin the regular fifty-fifty custody arrangement."

Langston nods. "That all sounds good to me. I'll have to get my house ready for him, but that's nothing Maggie, my assistant, can't handle."

Amanda nods. "That's what I'd hoped you'd say."

"Where are you getting your cancer treatments?" Langston asks.

"I'll be driving the thirty minutes over to Orchard Blossom to the cancer center at their hospital."

"That's the closest hospital," Laurie says. "It's a good choice. I've heard good things about their cancer center."

"So have I. I would have chosen to move closer to Atlanta if it weren't this good, so I'm glad it's working out."

"It's the middle of the school year. Are you putting Hayden in Blue Mountain Elementary?" I ask.

"Yes. I'll sign him up on Monday after spring break is over."

"Have you thought about a tutor?" Langston speaks up. We all grew up with tutors, so it would make sense that he would think of that. "I want my son to have the best education imaginable."

"No." Amanda scoffs. "Do I look like I have the money to hire a tutor?"

"We'd be willing to cover the expense, of course," Langston explains.

"He's going to Blue Mountain Elementary like any *normal* kid his age."

Langston gets another one of those frustrated looks on his face. "We can talk about it later."

"There's no need. He's going to Blue Mountain Elementary, and that's final. I want him to live as normal a life as possible before he gets swept up in the life you all live."

What's wrong with the way we live?

My heart squeezes in my chest to see Langston going through this. He's seeing his son in front of him, one he never knew existed before, and he has no parental rights. If he wants any, he'll have to get a lawyer and a paternity test.

I curl my hands into fists. The entire thing is infuriating. I want to stand up for Langston and fight for him. Which isn't normal for me. And for the first time ever, he's not my rival, but my teammate.

10

LANGSTON

*A*s we're wrapping up our conversation, I lean over to Jenni. "Where's Hayden?" She smells comforting, like lavender.

She leans over to me too, so close I can feel her breath hitting my cheek. "He went upstairs to play video games."

"Do you think he'd be okay with it if I went up there to talk to him?" My heart quickens to think about having a son and having a relationship with him.

A tingle runs down my spine, having her so near to me. The emotions of Hayden coming into my life, and having Jenni being so supportive by my side are intertwining, and I'm working to stuff all these feelings down so they don't overwhelm me.

"I think you might want to take it slow. But I'll go with you. I've had the chance to build a bit of a relationship with him in the few moments I've spent with him." She stands, and I follow.

To say I'm nervous about talking with him is a massive understatement. But he's my boy, something I can barely wrap my head around. I still can't deny the fact that he looks like me. How bizarre is that?

Jenni loops her arm through mine, her body moving against my side as we talk toward the back staircase. When we get to the stairs, she slides her arm down and reaches for my hand instead. Her small hand is warm in my larger one, and we climb the stairs together.

Hayden is on the couch with a controller in his hands. He's got a video game on the TV, and his character is jumping from platform to platform.

"Good choice," I say. "I've beaten that game three times now."

Hayden keeps his eyes on the screen. "Cool." His little cartoon guy bounces across a pit of lava. "Do you like video games too?"

"I have an entire room in my house dedicated to gaming with all the comfy chairs and controllers and a cabinet full of all the best snacks."

Hayden's eyes grow huge. "Can I come over and see what games you have?"

I smile. "Whenever you want."

"How about tomorrow?" His little face is eager. He

looks away from the screen to me, and his character runs off a cliff.

"I'm pretty sure I have tomorrow available." I wink at him.

I'm supposed to be having a work meeting tomorrow, but I'll have to text Maggie to clear the entire day for Hayden now.

"Cool. Is your house as big as this one? It's gigantic!"

I chuckle. "Not quite as big."

"You haven't even seen all the rooms here," I say. "Did you know my mom and dad have a swimming pool here?"

Hayden frowns, scrunching his nose in frustration. "My mom won't let me swim when it's this cold. I've tried asking, but she always says no."

"Well, I bet she'll let you swim in this one." Jenni grins at him. "Because it's an indoor pool."

This seems to perk him right up. "Really?" He bounces up and down on the couch cushion. But then he stops. "But I didn't bring a swimsuit." Another item to add to Maggie's shopping list.

"Don't you worry about that," I tell him. "I'll make sure you get one."

The smile returns to Hayden's face. It's good to see him getting excited about something simple like video games and swimming. At least it's distracting him from the fact that he has a new father in his life and a sick mom.

Or maybe making it into a positive experience for him.

"Dad?" Hayden asks after a moment of quiet. "Do you want to play with me? I think this game has two-player mode."

"Sure." I pick up a controller from the TV cabinet and take a seat next to Hayden.

I'm still not used to him calling me Dad, but I have a feeling I could adapt to this new life quite happily.

~

*A*fter Hayden is shown to his room and is tucked into bed, I turn to Jenni. "Would you be okay with coming to my house? I'm not sure I can sit at home alone right now."

"If you want. Let's just say goodbye to your mom first."

We head to the living room where she's sitting with a cup of tea by the fire. She looks up at us. Amanda's already retired to her room, so it's just the three of us. My dad was away on business in Singapore, so he missed the entire thing.

"Have you told Mr. Keith he has a new grandson?" Jenni asks, sitting next to her.

Mom shakes her head. "I haven't even had a chance yet. It's been an overwhelming night."

"I can't imagine getting a call like that."

"I don't know if he'll be happy or angry that Hayden has been kept from us all these years." Mom's keeping her voice low, because it wouldn't do to have Amanda or Hayden randomly show up and overhear what we're saying.

"I'd imagine both," Jenni says. "I'm angry for you."

I'm angry too, but the fact that Hayden is in my life now is overpowering that anger.

Mom sighs. "Yes. But there's no point in being angry now. The best thing we can do is love that boy."

"That's how I feel too." My heart swells at her words.

Jenni's face softens. "You're absolutely right."

"And support Langston all you can." Mom reaches over to grab my hand. "This will be hard for you."

"We're headed over to his house after this to help him process all of this." Jenni looks over at me with "love" in her eyes. I know it's an act for my mom, but strangely, I want it to be real. It's nice to have her support through all of this, even if it's just pretend.

Do we even need to put on an act anymore? Would it be possible that Mom would want me to get back together with Amanda to help her through her illness and for the sake of Hayden?

Mom gives Jenni a giant smile, like this news makes

her happy. "Now, don't you two get too carried away." She shakes a finger at me. "You'd better behave yourselves."

Whatever she thinks Jenni and I might be doing tonight will never happen. There's no way Jenni would allow it. I smile back at her. "Yes, ma'am." Because that's a promise I can keep.

Right? Surely Jenni's warmth toward me is just an act still.

As soon as the words are out of my mouth, doubt and nervousness creep in, circling around me until my heart begins to race and my palms dampen.

Jenni and I almost kissed this morning. If we're together alone at my place, who knows what might happen? But there won't be anyone to convince, and likely nothing will happen.

We say goodbye to my mom and head over to my place.

And I'm nervous. It's not a big deal. I've hung out with Jenni plenty of times. There's nothing to be worried about. But there was something real between us this morning, and I didn't imagine that. And with the upheaval of the night and seeing how wronged I was by Amanda, I need Jenni's support.

It's hard to know how she really feels about all of this.

When we get to my place and climb out of our cars, Jenni says, "Was that a crazy night or what?"

"Crazy is an understatement. I think this calls for a bottle of wine. Something special." I fetch the bottle of Chateau Cos d'Estournel that I've been saving for a special occasion.

She sees the bottle in my hands when I come back with it. "Oh, wow. You weren't kidding when you said it was something special."

"Getting a new son in my life is worth celebrating."

I tangle a couple of wine glasses between my fingers and bring them over to the coffee table next to where she's settled on the couch.

I uncork the wine and pour us each a glass.

I hold up my glass in a toast. "To my new son."

"Cheers to that."

We both sip the wine, and I savor it as the liquid travels down my throat. "That's divine." I moan.

She licks her lips and sets the glass down. "Some of the best I've had."

I can't help staring at the movement of her tongue flicking across her lips.

She places a hand on my knee, the warmth of her skin seeping into my slacks. "How are you doing with all this?"

"Truthfully? I'm caught in this place where I'm ecstatic to have a new son, but I can't help but feel angry at Amanda for the years she robbed from us." I cradle my glass between my hands. "My mind is racing with so many questions and possibilities, but mostly,

I'm just terrified. How am I supposed to raise a kid? What if I'm terrible at it? It's not like I raised him from birth, and he got the opportunity to bond with me. All of that has been ripped away from us." I don't want to get too bitter about it, but I'm angry.

"I would say Amanda must have had her reasons for keeping Hayden a secret from you, but I can't think of what they must have been to warrant what she did."

Her hair is swept back from her face except for one tendril that's escaped. She looks gorgeous today, as always. Dressed impeccably in a navy-and-white spotted blouse and navy pencil skirt that hugs her body, which is a big change from how she looked this morning, covered in mud. But strangely, she was even more beautiful that way. Wild and carefree, laughing. Looking at her pristine appearance now makes me wonder if she still has traces of mud beneath her fingernails, a telltale remnant of our mud fight earlier.

There's something new between us, and it's growing and changing by the minute. It all started with that almost kiss this morning. Even with everything going on today, I haven't forgotten it.

"Thank you for caring so much," I whisper, taking another sip of my wine before setting it on the table. I reach up and sweep back her renegade lock of hair.

She shudders under my touch, and our gazes lock. "Of course," she breathes.

Warmth fills my chest as I keep my attention on

her. "And thank you for being there tonight. I know you were just there for appearances' sake, but I needed it more than I realized."

"It was my pleasure." Her voice is sweet and sincere, and I want to kiss her, to feel her lips on mine, and entangle my hands in her hair.

Only, I don't know how she'd react. Would she pull away from me?

"If you need any help with Hayden, I'm here for you," she says, reaching out and rubbing the back of my neck, causing my breath to catch. "And I don't mean it as part of our act. I want to help you. I'm not an expert on parenting, but I love kids and I've grown pretty fond of Hayden already." She smiles, her eyes sparkling. "He has your dimples."

"You noticed that, huh?" my voice is low and husky, and I take another sip of wine. I need to calm my nerves and maybe take a little bit of the edge off of the day I've had.

She continues to rub my neck, and I sink into her touch, which feels like magic.

"I thought you didn't like me," I say.

Her hand kneads into my shoulders. "Who says I do?"

"Your hands seem to be saying they do."

"Oh? You like this?" Her voice is silky and low.

A shudder runs through me, and my senses are alive.

I grin, somehow still keeping my wits about me. "Don't get too cocky. You're still the enemy."

"Still bitter about Valentine winning?" Her eyes are playful now, and I suddenly want to keep them that way. She should always look like this. Happy, present in the moment, not a care in the world.

"Bitter is too strong of a word..." I trail off.

She gives me this knowing smile. "Is it though?"

"It's only making me that much more determined to win in the future. Valentine only won by a small margin. I plan to make sure that doesn't happen next time."

"And what if you're too distracted to put that level of effort in?" Her face is close to mine now, and I can hardly breathe.

"Distracted by what?" I murmur.

"I think you know." Her lips are scarcely an inch from mine, and I can't take it anymore. I close that inch and take her lips with mine. Gently and slowly, prodding and testing to see if it's really what she wants.

But then she puts a hand to the back of my neck and pulls me in closer. That's when I throw caution to the wind. I delve my hands into her hair and pull her closer to me too. This is more than just a playful kiss between friends. My heart is expanding in my chest, and I feel it binding and entwining with hers. All the years of being around Jenni, staying away from her but also admiring her, have combined to create this perfect moment. It was there all along, but I was never able to acknowledge it.

Her lips are sweet like honey, and they're soft and pliable beneath mine. She knows what she's doing too. Who knew Jenni could kiss so well? She's full of surprises today, and this is the good kind.

She's been faithfully by my side today, a strong emotional support on the most shocking day of my life. And it was more than an act. Jenni went above and beyond what she would need to do to sell the relationship thing. She was being a true friend to me. And that's the kind of person I want by my side. Someone on my team. Jenni and I would be a force together. Why hadn't I ever seen this beautiful truth before?

But then, Ronnie's angry face appears in my mind. Oh yeah. That's why. Because my best friend would kill me if he knew I was kissing his sister like this, without anyone around to convince. If he ever finds out about this moment, I'd have to face the worst of his wrath. And to make matters worse, Amanda is moving to Blue Mountain, which will be a constant reminder that I betrayed him by marrying the girl he'd fallen for.

I pull away. "I'm sorry, Jenni. We shouldn't have done that."

She opens her eyes and looks back at me. "Why not?"

"You know why not. Because of Ronnie."

She juts her chin out. "You think I care what he

thinks?" She crosses her arms. "I can kiss who I want. I don't need his permission."

"But I have to answer to him. He's my best friend, and I don't want to lose that friendship." I stand up.

"I should probably go," Jenni says.

"Right. Uh…" I rub the back of my neck. "Thanks for stopping by."

Jenni stands too. "Anytime. Please call me if you're having a hard time."

My heart aches to see her leave. I've probably hurt her by ending our kiss so abruptly, but it can't be helped.

The problem is, now that I've kissed Jenni, I'm not sure I'll ever be able to think of her the same. And we still have to pretend to be in love in front of all our family members.

How am I supposed to keep my distance emotionally while keeping her close physically for the public eye?

11

JENNI

*L*angston is right. Our kiss was a mistake. The fake romance is turning real, and I'm not prepared for that. I didn't think it would happen. Langston and me? Nah.

But that kiss was on fire. The tension between Langston and me has been heating up, and I'd gotten to the point that I wanted the kiss. A little too much. Falling for Langston was never part of the plan. This was supposed to be a fake romance, not a real one. Because now there are feelings involved, and that makes this complicated.

Langston is the kind of guy I could see myself with long term. I could see us getting serious and quickly. We already have both our parents rooting for us. Everyone already thinks we're an item. So why not just let it be real?

Because Langston deserves a woman who can have the babies his mom wants from him. That woman could never be me. Sure, he has Hayden now, but he's going to want to hold his future children in his arms as newborns. That was taken from him. If anything permanent ever happened between us, I couldn't give that to him.

Today is Langston's first day alone with Hayden, and it's all I can think about while I'm at work. Well, technically, I'm at home in my office, but as soon as I cross into that room, it counts as being at work. Otherwise, I'm distracted all day with a million little things. I still struggle with being distracted, but I've learned to put my phone down during working hours unless I'm using it for actual company phone calls. That strategy has helped me find a lot of success.

Around four, I get a call I can't take, and when I check my voicemail, it's from the foster care people. They want to set up a time to meet with me. My heart lifts. I could really make a difference in some kids' lives. I want that more than anything. I want to help more than just babies; older kids have a harder time getting adopted.

I might not be able to have my own kids, but I have so much to give—all this love and no one to shower it on, not any kids anyway. But there is Hayden. I think the two of us are going to be buddies. Now that's a child I could grow to love. I've known him one day, and I think he's already stolen a little corner of my heart. That little stinker.

I wonder how he's getting along with his dad on their first visitation day...

After work, I change into jeans and boots and head to my parents' house. I call on my way over to request that Marshmallow get saddled up. Riding Marshmallow over to Langston's property will allow me to scope out how those two are doing. I wouldn't mind bonding with the little guy some more. Sure, I could drive, but I'm in the mood for a ride after the emotional day I've had trying to bottle up my feelings for Langston. And trying to ignore the instant replay of that kiss that keeps popping up in my thoughts.

It was the best kiss of my life, hands down. And that's what makes this so dangerous. I can't allow myself to get too close to Langston because I don't want to end up hurting him in the end. I'm no good for him. I'm broken. I know I should be happy the way I am. With my great career, it shouldn't matter that I can't have kids, but it's so ingrained in me that one day I'd be giving my parents grandbabies that I can't help but feel this way.

The spring air smells sweet, like fresh blossoms. The leaves are sprouting on the trees now. It's the perfect time for Hayden to be introduced to Blue

Mountain. It's beautiful year-round, but spring is one of the most gorgeous times of year. The dogwoods are blooming their white flowers, and pink fringe is popping up on the redbud trees.

Marshmallow is saddled up when I get to my parents' house, and Valentine is out working with the trainer again to prepare for the Blue Mountain Derby.

I'm a little nervous about the race since Thunder was so close to beating Valentine, and then Langston admitted he was working extra hard to win the next one.

Just because I've kissed Langston, and it was toe-curling, doesn't mean I'm willing to let him win.

I prod Marshmallow forward, and we pick up speed, the wind rushing through my hair as we fly across the field. Adrenaline pumps through my body. There's not a roller coaster out there that could give me as much of a thrill as riding Marshmallow. And I love amusement parks. The scarier the ride, the better.

I hit Langston's property at full speed and slow as I head down the trail that leads to his stable. He has a ton of acreage for a guy his age. But when you have the kind of money he has, you can do virtually whatever you want with it. Even if you want your own horse racing track on your land.

When I reach the stables, Langston and Hayden are out there. I haven't told them I was planning to come over, so it's a coincidence that they are doing horse stuff today too. Well, maybe not that much coincidence. Langston and I are equally obsessed with riding and all things horse related.

Hayden and Langston are both wearing cowboy hats, and I can't help wondering where they found a cowboy hat for him.

Hayden looks up to see me, and his face lights up from beneath the brim of his hat. "Hi, Lady-I-Don't-Remember-The-Name-Of."

"Oh, it looks like you've inherited your father's dimples as well as his sense of humor. My name's Jenni."

"Huh?" Hayden pokes at his face with both fingers. "I have his dimples?"

"It was the first thing I noticed about you." I swing down from Marshmallow's back. "Langston, show him."

Langston smiles at Hayden, and his face lights up. "Hey! Those do look like mine."

It's incredible to see him so pleased to look like his dad. He's surprised us all by how well he's adjusting to having Langston in his life.

"Have you ever ridden a horse before, Hayden?" I ask.

He shakes his head. "Nope."

"We were just talking about him trying it out." Langston reaches up to pet Dash.

"Daisy is a good one for him to start with." I point

to the chestnut mare chewing on hay lazily in her stall. "She's a really sweet horse. I think you'll like her, Hayden."

"Sweet?" He wrinkles his nose. "I want a fast one, like Thunder."

Langston laughs. "You'd better stick to a horse like Daisy. Only the jockey rides Thunder."

I look over at Langston. "You told him you race horses?"

"We were just starting to talk about it when you showed up," Langston says.

"Did he tell you we have a big race coming up?" I ask, bending down to Hayden's level.

"Yeah, the Blue Mountain Derby, and he's racing against your horse, Mushroom."

"Marshmallow," I correct. "And Marshmallow isn't my racehorse. It's Valentine."

"Oh, marshmallows are a much yummier food." Hayden grins. "Hey, Dad? Can we have s'mores?"

"I think we can make that happen," Langston says. "Have you ever been camping before?"

"No. My mom hates bugs, so she's never taken me."

This poor kid. He's missed out on so much by not having a dad around. Every eight-year-old needs to experience camping with their dad.

"Would you like to go?" I ask. "Because I happen to love camping, and Langston has a lot of land. There's even a cool camping spot we like to go to. Usually, he goes with my brother Ronnie, but sometimes they let me tag along too."

Hayden's eyes get big and round. "Really? Do you think my mom would let me?"

"We can ask her," Langston says. "But if she says no, we can't argue with her."

Wow. I respect a man who can get along with his ex. But if it were me, I'd be wanting to stir up drama with her. I'm ready to pull out the boxing gloves with this woman. She drives me nuts. But Langston is a bigger person than I am, apparently. "But if she does say yes, we can take the horses to the campsite."

Fear sweeps across his features. "Well...I'm not sure... I mean..."

"Do you want to try it out with Daisy?" Langston offers.

"You're not scared, are you?" I ask. "I thought you were just saying you want a fast horse." It's like he was being all bravado a minute ago, but now that he's actually facing riding to the camp out, the fear is sinking in.

"Maybe a little," he admits, pulling his shoulders up to his ears.

"Well, let's give it a shot," Langston says. "But you're wearing a helmet." He pulls out one of the kid ones he keeps around from when he has friends with kids come over to ride. They swap the cowboy hat for the helmet and strap it under his chin.

Once Daisy is saddled up, Langston lifts Hayden onto her back.

Seeing him together with his son like this is doing funny things to my insides, and I realize I want to be a part of this. I fit with them. Flashes of Hayden growing older with Langston and me standing side by side watching go through my mind. We could go on so many adventures, make so many memories.

Instead of mounting Marshmallow, I lead Daisy around the field, walking in front slowly, so Hayden can get used to the feel of the horse under him. The kid is a natural.

"This isn't as scary as I thought it would be," Hayden says. "Can we go a little faster?"

"How about you try walking a bit on your own?" Langston says.

"Oh, alright," Hayden complains.

I show him how to control the horse, and he takes off on his own, Langston following at a safe distance with Dash.

I head back to where I'd left Marshmallow tied up and climb on his back, riding over to where Langston is.

"Where'd you find the cowboy hat for him?" I ask after pulling alongside him.

"We went out shopping today and found it at Anna's Gift Shop."

"That place has the cutest stuff." Once I'd gotten

my mom a tea set from there. "I thought you'd had Maggie go out and find it for you."

"No, we just kind of stumbled across it when we were out. I was showing him around Blue Mountain with my mom. And you know how she is. She has to go in that gift shop every time she's in town."

I laugh because I do know. She probably provides half that store's revenue. "So whose idea was it to buy Hayden the hat?" I ask.

Langston arches a brow at me. "Do you really have to ask that?"

I laugh. "Your mom?"

"Bingo. She's dying to get that boy to feel welcome in our family."

"There's nothing wrong with that."

"Didn't say there was. I just don't want to push him too fast." He's keeping his voice down, and Hayden is far enough ahead of us to be out of earshot.

"But he was wearing the hat earlier," I point out. "That's a good sign, right?"

"I suppose." He takes off his own hat and runs a hand through his hair. "I just don't want to mess this up. I'm not exactly ready for all this dad stuff. I have no idea what I'm doing here."

"Hey." I want to reach over to put a comforting hand on him, but he's too far away. "Is anyone ever ready to be a parent?"

"I don't know."

"From what I've heard, there's nothing that can prepare you. Not really. You just have to live it and wing it the entire time."

"Maybe there's a class I can take or something."

My mind immediately goes to the foster parenting classes I'm required to take before I can have a child placed in my home. Maybe something like that could help Langston too. I know his situation is different, and that he's likely not looking to take on foster kids, but maybe there's a similar class he could take—or... that's it!

"What about trying family therapy? You could have someone come into your home and work with you guys."

"I don't know. It might be a bit too much for Hayden."

"It's just an idea." I shrug. "Either way, I'd bet Hayden's going to need a bunch of therapy to sort out all of the new changes in his life."

"I wonder if his mom would be okay with that," Langston says.

"I don't know her well enough to say either way."

"Can I go faster now, Dad?" Hayden calls back to us.

"Maybe you should keep it slower for now. You've barely tried riding that horse."

"Come on. I can handle it," Hayden whines.

Langston looks over at me and smiles. "This is what I have to look forward to for the rest of my life."

"Well, at least until he's eighteen," I point out.

"Nah, you should see my brothers. They're still trying to get my mom to let them do all kinds of crazy things that she won't allow."

I raise my brow at him. "Your brothers? How about you? You're the worst one out of all of them."

He laughs because he knows I'm right. "My point is, I like this dad stuff. It's scary and I'm sure it will be tough at times, but the good parts, like right now, show me how wonderful being a dad can be."

My heart tugs at his words. Why does that make me like him so much more? I'm not supposed to let my heart get involved, but now it's melting and it's not like I can help it. The guy is acting all tender with Hayden, and it's hard not to get pulled in by it.

"Hayden's a natural on that horse," I say. "He takes after you."

"That's what my mom's been saying all day," Langston says, keeping his gaze on Hayden. "She wants to take him out shopping tomorrow for new clothes."

"What's wrong with the clothes he has?" I ask.

"Nothing. But you know my mom. She's just looking for an excuse to spoil him. She's waited a long time for this."

I can't help but laugh. "That does sound about right."

Langston's eyes soften as he looks out at Hayden, and my heart flutters. Watching them together is melting my heart, and I only want to spend time with them even more.

12

LANGSTON

We approach Amanda at my parents' house after our riding session when it's time to return Hayden to his mom for the night.

"Mom, can I please go camping with Dad and Jenni? They said we can take horses to the campsite and everything."

She looks between us. "Are you sure you're ready for a big step like this?" He still hasn't spent the night with me yet, and Amanda had planned on him spending several days with me until spring break is over.

"As long as it's all right with your dad, I don't see why you can't go. When did you want to do it?"

"I was thinking tomorrow night. School starts back up on Monday, and this could be a fun way to finish off his spring break." I love how he invited Jenni along. I glance over at her. "Would you like to come with us?"

She glows at the invitation. "I'd love to. That sounds really fun."

And now it feels like we're about to be one big happy family, and I can't help the way it's making my heart grow warm. I'm falling more for this woman every day but acting like we're a family has it on a whole other level.

~

Friday night, we set out on horseback to the campsite. Our favorite place to go camping is way back on my parents' land, about a mile's ride. We've packed all our supplies onto the horses.

"Is this how the cowboys did it back in the day?" Hayden asks just after we've taken off down the trail. The trees are just starting to get their leaves, and it's warmer today than it's been lately.

"I'm sure there are still cowboys camping this way. Just look at us," I point out. "We count as cowboys, right?"

Jenni looks over at us and smiles. "All you have to do is wear a cowboy hat, and it magically makes you a cowboy. Didn't you know that?"

I laugh. "Well, technically, a cowboy is someone

who rides in a rodeo or works at a ranch herding cattle. But we've gotten a little looser with the terminology over the years. But all good cowboys are kind to others and work hard. We can get the job done, no matter how hard it may be."

"And love riding horses," Hayden says. "Have you ever had cows, Dad?"

My heart still does funny things in my chest when he calls me that. I know I'll get used to it eventually, but it's still shiny and new. "I had some old dairy cows when I was younger. They were my parents', but they haven't had any in a while. These days, we're all about the horses."

"Remember Betsy, the old cranky milk cow your parents had when we were kids?" Jenni asked.

"Oh, she wasn't cranky. She was sweet."

"That's not how I remember it," Jenni says. "I got kicked more than once when I tried to milk her."

"Usually, we let the machines milk her, but you insisted on trying it by hand right after she'd had a calf," I remind her. "A cow who's used to the machines will freak out if you try to milk her by hand," I explain to Hayden.

"Then why did your parents let you milk her by hand?" Hayden asks.

"Well..." How do I tell my kid about how I was sneaky and didn't let them know Jenni and I were milking cows without permission?

Jenni and I lock gazes and a small smile flits across her face. "She was cranky more than once," Jenni insists, changing the subject. "It was all the time."

"Nah," I say. "Only during her time of the month."

Jenni laughs, but Hayden looks over with a confused expression. "What time of the month?"

Heat creeps across my face. Did I just bring up this topic in front of my son? "You know, the birds and the bees?" His mom gave him that talk, right? Wait, he's only eight. Some kids get that talk when they're older. First, I almost tell him how I got into trouble as a kid, and now this?

Hayden looks even more confused. "What do birds and bees have to do with the cow?"

Jenni can't hold her laughter back anymore. "Yeah, Langston. Why don't you explain all of this to Hayden?"

I'm in deep doo-doo now. "I, uh, well..."

Jenni enjoys my floundering a minute longer before coming to the rescue. "You'll have to ask your mom about it when we get back."

"Okay." And by the determined look on his face, I don't doubt that he'll be having that conversation.

Before long, we arrive at the campsite, and I swing down from Dash's back. Hayden wriggles in his saddle like he's trying to figure out how to get down.

"Hold on there, buddy. Let me help you." I lift him out of his saddle and gently ease him to the ground. A wave of protectiveness comes over me, and it hits me that I'd do anything for this boy. I haven't really held him like this before. Well, I did when I helped him on and off of the horses before, but this is the first time I've really felt this protectiveness. He's small and needs a dad in his life, something that every kid needs. And I haven't been able to be there for him before this, but now I promise myself that I'll always be there for him from now on. I don't care how demanding work may become. This boy will be my top priority.

We tie Marshmallow, Dash, and Daisy up to some trees and get busy unloading our gear.

"Want to help me set up the tent?" I ask Hayden.

"Yeah!"

Hayden and I set up the tent together, and Jenni sets up hers across from ours.

"Why can't Jenni sleep with us?" Hayden asks me.

"Well, she's a girl. She has to sleep in the girl tent."

"I thought you said Jenni was your girlfriend."

"She is."

"My mom sleeps in bed with her different boyfriends all the time. Or at least she used to. She hasn't had a boyfriend in a long time. I think it's because she's sick."

I meet Jenni's gaze. She presses her lips together but doesn't say anything.

"Well, Jenni and I do things differently, and that's okay. Everyone does things their own way."

Hayden seems to accept this, and we move on to staking the tent into the ground.

Once the tents are up, Hayden looks over at me. "Now what?"

I grin. "It will be dark soon. How about we get a campfire started? I have hot dogs and marshmallows we can roast over the fire."

Hayden jumps up and down. "Yes, yes, yes!" It warms my heart to see him having fun. He's been through a lot. With Amanda cycling through who knows how many guys, it had to be hard on him. And it's only gotten harder since her diagnosis, I'm sure.

"First, we need to gather the wood," Jenni says. There's a pile of logs that we keep stowed near the campsite, but we still need smaller sticks for kindling.

I show Hayden the sizes of sticks we need, and he happily sets off, collecting them.

"He loves this," Jenni says with her eyes on him.

"Maybe we can get him in Cub Scouts or something," I suggest. "Or at least some sort of summer camp."

Jenni gives a soft laugh. "We?"

My face heats up. "Well, er... I just said that, huh? I guess I'm thinking of a future for us already. This feels real to me, Jenni."

"I know what you mean. It feels reals to me too."

Hearing Jenni say that sends fireworks exploding

inside me. I want to take her in my arms and kiss her until her toes curl.

Jenni clears her throat. "Do you even know what kind of extracurriculars he's tried?"

I shake my head. "There's still so much about him I don't know."

"Well, he told me he loves animals and wants to be a vet one day," Jenni says.

"Maybe we can take him to visit the pet shelter or something."

Hayden bends to get a stick that's about five feet long.

"That one might be a little big for our fire." I cross the campsite to where he's struggling with the unruly branch.

"We can chop it up with an axe," Hayden says.

"I'm afraid I'm fresh out of axes." And Amanda wouldn't be too happy about me giving her kid sharp, dangerous objects anyway. "But I have an idea." I prop it up against a fallen tree. "Come jump on this, Hayden."

He's more than happy to oblige. He pounces on the poor branch until it's broken in lots of small pieces. "How 'bout them apples?" he exclaims.

Jenni and I laugh. "Where does he come up with this stuff?" Jenni says, shaking her head.

I crouch in the dirt with Hayden near the fire ring and teach him how to arrange the sticks in a formation that's conducive to keeping a flame alive. "There you go," I say once it's caught fire. "You're officially a camper now."

"Almost." Jenni crouches beside us. "We have to see if he can make it through the night."

"Are you sure you can stay out here all night?" I ask Hayden. "It can get pretty scary out here when it's all dark and Gordon the Ghoul is wandering about."

"Who's Gordon the Ghoul?" Hayden asks, settling onto one of the logs around the campfire.

"You've never heard of him?" I lean closer to Hayden. "You know, Jenni here is terrified of him," I stage whisper.

"You're going to frighten the boy with those spooky stories," Jenni scolds.

"I'm not scared." Hayden puffs his chest out, all bravado. "I want to hear about Gordon."

Jenni brings over a package of hotdogs and a couple of roasting sticks, the kind that retract to get really small and easily transportable. She extends them and stabs a hotdog onto one before handing it to Hayden.

"Did you know there was once gold discovered in these mountains?" I ask.

Hayden's eyes get huge. "Is that how you guys got so rich?"

I chuckle. "No. My family never discovered any, but one of Jenni's ancestors did back in the early 1800s in a nearby town in Georgia called Dahlonega. And so did Gordon."

Jenni hands me a roasting stick with a hotdog perched on the end, and I poke it into the flames, with her doing the same from her end of the fire.

"What happened to him?" Hayden asks.

"Well, he wasn't the smartest guy. Gordon went around town yelling that he found gold. Some of the men who didn't find any gold snuck into his house while he was sleeping and stole all of his gold. And to this day, they say that Gordon haunts these woods, angry about his stolen gold."

"Did Jenni's family steal the gold?" Hayden whispers to me.

I shake my head. "No, it turns out it was his brother. Jenni's ancestors found their gold fair and square."

"How did he find out it was his brother?"

"All of a sudden, he had all this money. He dressed in the best clothes and spent all the money on ..." I was going to say on gambling and women, but Hayden doesn't need the less kid friendly parts of the story. "Well, let's just say he wasted away all the money. And Gordon has been furious about it ever since. A few people have seen Gordon hanging around these woods. Legend says that he haunts Jenni's family because he's jealous that they got all the money."

Jenni waves a hand dismissively. "That's not true. Don't listen to him, Hayden."

"She's in denial. Either that or she doesn't want to admit how scared she really is inside." I look over to Hayden, who seems to be hanging on my every word. "Did you know that we spooked her one time when we were kids out here camping? Jenni was so scared she peed her pants."

"I did not!" Jenni scowls at me. "Don't listen to anything he's saying, Hayden. He's just full of nonsense."

Hayden grins and leans over to me and whispers, "I think we should prank her tonight."

"I like how you think," I whisper back to him.

"It would be really funny if she peed her pants again."

"What are you two talking about over there?" Jenni eyes us with suspicion.

"Oh, nothing," Hayden says innocently. "Dad was just telling me a little more about Gordon the Ghoul." Even in the darkness, I can see his dimples popping as he smiles at Jenni, like he's not up to anything at all.

This kid is definitely my son. He even knows to team up with me against Jenni.

After eating hotdogs and s'mores, it's time to roll out our sleeping bags and hit the hay.

Jenni goes into her tent, but then re-emerges in pink fuzzy pajama pants with hearts all over them and a pink-and-black hoodie. Usually, Jenni is polished with every hair in place. Even when she's riding, she has her hair pulled back neatly. It's nice to see her a bit more casual. It's been a long time since I've seen her in pajamas. Jenni brushes her teeth and rinses her mouth with a drink from a water bottle.

There's something so intimate about seeing her this way. And those pants are begging me to snuggle up with her. It's a good thing Ronnie doesn't know we're on this campout together. He wouldn't know it was Hayden's idea to bring Jenni along and wouldn't see a reason for me to bring her, since I'm not actually dating her. But the truth is, I wanted Jenni to come, and not because I had to keep up some act. No, I wanted her company because I actually like her and want to spend time with her. And let's be honest, I'm kind of hoping for another kiss from her at some point.

But if Hayden or Mom or someone else mentions to Ronnie that I'm camping with his sister and my son and no one else, he probably won't like it.

"Dad, are you going to kiss her?" I turn to see Hayden studying me. He must have caught me staring at Jenni with who knows what kind of look on my face.

"Well..."

Jenni looks over at me with a crooked smile. "There's nothing to be scared of, Langston. My breath is fresh." She waves her toothbrush at me and then crooks her finger for me to approach her.

I look from her to Hayden and then back again. If I don't kiss her, Hayden will think something is wrong between us, and he might repeat that to my mom or his mom even. But Jenni looks like she's ready and willing.

So I go to her. She smiles up at me, and it hits me in the gut like a punch and dazzles me. I bend my head down to her, breathing in her lavender scent. It's a little worn off now that we're in the woods, but the woodsy fresh-air smell of her is just as enticing.

I hesitate for a moment with just a fraction of air between us. "I won't bite, Langston. I promise," she whispers to me.

"It's not you I'm afraid of."

"Just play along," she murmurs.

So I comply. Just throw me in that briar patch. Her lips are soft and warm, but pliable beneath mine. Something clicks into place, and this moment feels so right. I want to run my hands through her hair, pull her toward me. If I could, I'd stay like this forever until our hearts knit together and I could show her the way she deserves to be cherished. Because she is amazing —smart, funny, driven—even if she can be a bit too competitive at times. But I wouldn't change that about her. It's part of the draw.

"Eww. Gross, you guys."

We pull apart, laughing. "You're the one who wanted me to kiss her," I say.

"No way! I just wanted to know if you were going to. That doesn't mean I wanted you to. Ick!"

"Hayden, this is what boyfriends and girlfriends do," Jenni tells him.

"I know, I know. But it's still gross."

"You won't mind it so much when you're older," I say.

After all these years, who would have thought that I'd be proving my family right after all the times they told me I should date Jenni. I know it's still technically fake, but every day I'm with Jenni it's starting to feel more and more real.

And after that kiss, I'm wondering if maybe I can talk some sense into Ronnie, after all. Because this woman is stealing my heart more and more.

Hayden heads to bed, and Jenni and I sit around the campfire together. Jenni's wrapped in a plaid blanket, and she looks so snuggly. I want to take her in my arms and kiss her more, but I don't.

"I really like you, Jenni. I may have been competitive with you over the racetrack, but I've always thought you were incredible. The only thing stopping me from being with you now is Ronnie."

"I hate that. Ronnie isn't in charge of me." Jenni sounds angrier than before when we talked about this.

"I don't want to make you upset. The point is, I want to be with you, and Ronnie is a concern."

"I like you too, Langston. But if you knew everything about me, you'd probably change your mind about wanting to be with me." Her face is pained in the firelight.

"What do you mean?"

She presses her lips together. "It's late. We should probably get some sleep." She gets up and leaves me hanging.

Now my mind is racing as she retreats into her tent.

What could possibly be wrong with Jenni, who seems perfect and wonderful in every way?

13

JENNI

I jolt awake. The woods are silent around my tent, and I can't tell what might have woken me up. But my heart is racing. "Langston?"

There's no sound, and now my skin is starting to crawl. I sit up in my sleeping bag and rub my eyes. My phone says it's three in the morning. I sigh and lay back down. Maybe I was just having a bad dream that I can't remember now.

But then there's a scratching sound on the side of my tent coming from the outside.

"Langston? Are you guys awake?"

Neither Langston or Hayden respond, and now I'm getting freaked out.

Then as I wake more, my mind clears, and I remember that I'd overheard Langston and Hayden plotting to play pranks on me. I open my sleeping bag silently and slither out of it and crouch next to the tent wall where the noise has been coming from. I growl ferociously and shake the tent like it's an earthquake. I expect to hear them scream or giggle or something, but there's only a scrambling sound, rustling the leaves on the ground around the tent.

"Very funny, you guys. The joke's up. I'm not buying your spooky nonsense."

But they're still silent, other than more rustling.

"Jenni?" It's Langston's voice, but it's not coming from near my tent. It's coming from a way's off and is muffled like his voice may be coming from inside his tent.

"Are you outside my tent, Langston?" I ask.

"No, why do you ask?" His voice sounds rough, like he's just woken up. Then I hear a small groan, like Hayden's just been woken up too.

"Uhh, if you're not out here, then who is?"

"I thought you said Gordon the Ghoul was just pretend," Hayden says, sleep still heavy in his voice.

"He is, but whatever's out here is very much alive and kicking."

"Do you need me to come out and rescue you?" Langston calls to me.

"Maybe we should all just stay where we are," I say. The last thing I want is to have a bear attack me.

But then the scratching is back, and now I know I'm doomed. I scream, hoping the bear gets scared by it and runs off. But all I hear is laughing. And I'd know that laugh anywhere.

"Ronnie! What are you doing out here at three in the morning?" I unzip my tent to find my brother bent over laughing and Langston and Hayden standing outside the tent. Ronnie clicks on his flashlight, and I can see that Langston's hair is sticking up in a million different directions, which is pretty cute. Hayden is next to him with a similar hairstyle, again like father, like son.

"I got you good!" Ronnie says. "I scratched on the boys' tent first, but they never woke up. These two sleep like logs."

"Why are you out here so late?" I ask.

He shrugs. "I couldn't sleep, and I heard you guys were on a campout without inviting me. I figured a little revenge was in order."

Langston's face is full of fear in the glow of Ronnie's flashlight. Why would he be scared about Ronnie crashing our party?

"Is that all you're mad about?" Langston asks.

"We don't need to talk about this in front of your kid."

"You scared me to death, Ronnie!" I settle on a log next to the fire ring. I shiver in the night air, wishing for my sleeping bag. I'm still wearing my hoodie, at least.

Ronnie's face is like stone in the glimmer of light

being cast from the flashlight Langston's just turned on. Could it be that Ronnie knows there's more going on between us than just an act?

"It's cold out here," Hayden complains. "I'm going back to my sleeping bag."

Langston stokes the fire and gets it going again. "I can't believe you came all the way out here. Did you ride a horse?"

"Nope, I just walked."

"How did you even know we were out here?" Langston settles on a log next to me.

"How do you think? Our moms were going on and on about it at dinner tonight. How the three of you are like a happy family now and all their dreams are coming true. I came out here to make sure this is still fake because it seems awfully real now."

I look over at Langston, and he meets my gaze. Langston turns back to Ronnie. "You're right. It is real. I don't want to lose my friendship with you, Ronnie, but I can't stay away from Jenni either. Not when I feel this strongly about her."

Take my breath away already, Langston. Hearing him stick up for us like that makes me want him all the more.

"What?" Ronnie's voice is menacing and seems a little shocked that his hunch was correct. "You promised this was going to be fake, Langston. I told you not to mess with my sister, and you did exactly the opposite."

"Hey, I'm not messing with her. I'm treating her with the respect she deserves."

"The same respect you gave me when you stole Amanda away from me?"

"I can't change the past, Ronnie," Langston says. "And keep your voice down. Hayden is right in that tent. I don't want you yelling stuff about his mom in front of him."

"Ronnie, there's nothing wrong with Langston. And if you like him so much, then why shouldn't I be allowed to date him?" I don't intend to let things go too far with Langston, but that should be my choice, not Ronnie's. It has nothing to do with him.

"Langston took Amanda from me. What's to say he won't betray you in the end too?"

"That was a long time ago, Ronnie. Why can't you just forgive and forget?" I ask.

Ronnie crosses his arms and glares at Langston stubbornly. "If you don't stay away from my sister, we're through." He gets up, clicks on his flashlight, and heads down the path toward home.

Once he's out of earshot, Langston says in a lowered voice, "If Ronnie wants to alienate himself from us, then so be it. I'm not going to let him come between us." Langston takes my hand. "We just need to keep working on him. He'll come around when he realizes he can't change our minds."

"I agree. He's just being hardheaded right now."

Langston's eyes soften. "You're worth fighting for."

My chest grows warm at his words. "I don't deserve a guy as great as you. I don't care about what happened between you and Ronnie. It was almost a decade ago. Who cares?"

Langston gives a little laugh. "Ronnie apparently."

I grin. "Ronnie just needs a girl of his own. He won't care nearly as much if he has a wife bossing him around. The guy has too much time on his hands."

"You're getting to be as bad as my mom," Langston says.

"I think she's been a bad influence on me," I joke.

He takes my hands in his and rubs his thumbs over the backs of my hands. "She convinced you I was worth dating—or whatever this is between us."

"No, you convinced me of that all on your own."

He lets go of my hands and brushes my hair back from my face before kissing me. It's short and sweet, and he pulls back, keeping his gaze on mine.

"I like whatever this is between us," I whisper.

"I have to admit, it's a lot stronger than I thought it might be. I thought we'd just be having this silly fake dating thing, but I'm falling for you hard, Jenni."

My pulse speeds up as I take in the tender look in

his eyes. I can see the love and adoration shining through them. *Love?* Is that what I'm seeing?

It certainly feels like what I'm experiencing. I've known Langston for so long, always secretly admired his outward appearance and laughed with him over the years. He's almost been like family. But never quite. I've always been acutely aware of how attractive he is. How could I not be? But now? It's only been just over a week that we've been fake dating, and it already feels so real. Maybe it's been there, under the surface all this time. But I can't hide it any longer, and I don't want to.

"I've already fallen, Langston. I've never felt like this before, and it's scary and exciting all at the same time."

"I want to build a life with you," he says. "The whole nine yards, marriage, a whole houseful of kids. You're so good with Hayden. You'll make such a great mom one day."

A whole houseful of kids? That could be a possibility if we have foster children, but I don't think that's what Langston has in mind. I've come to accept my fate and am excited about my little dream of being a foster mom, but will that be enough for Langston? With Hayden, he missed out on those first eight years. Amanda took that away from him, but I can't take it from him too.

I shake my head. "I don't think I can."

"Why not? Does this have to do with what you were talking about earlier?"

I've never told anyone my secret, but I can't keep it hidden any longer. Langston deserves to know the truth. And then he'll break it off between us. It's better to end things now than to fall even harder and end up even more damaged.

"I can't give you the family you deserve."

"What are you talking about?"

"All those babies that you're dreaming of." Tears are forming in my eyes, and my throat is thickening.

"Why wouldn't you be able to make that happen? I thought you wanted kids one day." Langston looks thoroughly confused.

I take a deep breath and let it out. "I do. But I can't have them."

"What? Are you sure?" Langston's voice is gentle now, almost comforting, and it's making it worse because it's like he feels sorry for me, and I'm not sure I can handle that.

I nod miserably. "I'm positive. I've seen the doctor, and I'm unable to bear children."

Langston takes my hand. "I'm sorry, Jenni."

And now I'm crying. I wipe the tears away. I'm sleep deprived and emotional. It's not the best time to have this conversation, but is there ever a good time to tell the man you're in love with that you can't have his babies?

"I had no idea you've been carrying this around. Do your parents know?"

I shake my head. "No one knows." I wipe away a stray tear that's escaped.

"I don't know what to say. I want to fix this for you, but I can't. Have you tried everything? Or gotten a second opinion?"

"I can't. I don't want to hear bad news over and over. I've decided to become a foster parent instead."

"That's a wonderful thing to do. Think of all the kids you could help. With your resources, you could make a huge impact."

I nod. "I know. I've just scratched the surface. I'm supposed to meet with someone next week to find out more about the process."

"I think that's wonderful."

"But you deserve to hold your own baby in your arms one day," I say.

Langston is quiet for a moment, and I'm dying to know what's going through his mind.

"Why don't we call it a night, get some sleep, and we'll talk about this more in a bit?"

"That's not going to fix what's wrong with me." I'm getting emotional again, and I don't know how to stop it. I've been holding this inside for so long, and now that I've shared it with the man I've fallen for, it's like a floodgate has opened. My tears are falling freely now, and I can't fall apart in front of Langston. "I'm sorry. I have to go."

I rush off to my tent before Langston can stop me. I leave him to tend to the fire, and I crawl back into my sleeping bag, curling up into a fetal position. I shouldn't have told him. Because now, he's going to be the white knight and sacrifice his future happiness for my sake. I can't let that happen. He deserves better. I'm successful in so many ways, but I can't fix this one. And it's too hard to bear. My heart aches, and I sob into my pillow silently so Langston doesn't hear and come to the rescue. He doesn't need to know how much this is hurting me.

But now my heart has gotten involved. It's too late to prevent the hurt that I was hoping to avoid. Because it's consuming me. The only choice left is to break off things with Langston.

I don't care if my parents want to set me up with a guy in India. How can I care about that when my heart is hurting so much?

Maybe the answer is to tell my parents the truth about my infertility. I've tried all this time to protect them from the pain, and I've been holding it inside, putting on a brave front. But the burden is too heavy to bear now. Not with a broken heart thrown into the mix.

This campout was going so well before Ronnie crashed it. I wish he'd just stayed away. Why does he have to try to ruin everything? But the truth is, it's not really Ronnie's fault. My body is unable to bear children, regardless.

Ronnie is worried about protecting me from Langston. The truth is, he can't protect me from the real pain.

It's something I'm going to have to deal with on my own. If Ronnie only knew how strong I've had to be, he wouldn't feel this brotherly urge to save me somehow.

I guess it's sweet in its own way, but it would be nice too if he just learned that I'm capable of watching my own back.

14

LANGSTON

We break camp early in the morning and ride back to my parents' house to grab some breakfast. Jenni is eerily quiet all morning. Not exactly rude, but not warm either. It's as though she's detached from her emotions. Like a bomb is about to go off.

I'm getting the impression that there's nothing I can say to reassure her. I can't imagine how much pain she's been in as she's been hiding this big secret. She's only made things worse for herself by not telling anyone. Her parents would probably back off about her getting married. They'd likely allow her to date at her own pace. And maybe she'll never want to get married.

"That was the funnest campout ever." Hayden is

cheerful and hasn't seemed to notice that Jenni is more withdrawn than usual.

We'd planned to scare Jenni, but Hayden was asleep by the time I said goodnight to Jenni, and then Ronnie beat us to it. It's not the first time we've pranked Jenni on a campout, so Ronnie has gotten pretty good at it over the years.

"I'm glad you had fun. We'll have to do it again," I say. "But there are so many other things we can do together too." If Amanda would let us get him a tutor, we could do even more of the fun things I have in mind. He could have a much better education traveling the world and seeing different cultures and historical monuments than he would if he were sitting at a desk bored, day after day.

I have the means to give him the best education imaginable, but I have no parental rights. That's one of the first things that's going to change. I'll make a phone call to my lawyer as soon as I get Hayden distracted. Spending time with him these past few days has been better than I could have ever imagined. Amanda says she wants to have split custody with me, but what if we don't take the time to fill out the correct paperwork, she passes away (heaven forbid), and one of her family members try to swoop in and take Hayden? Everything has to be done by the book. Now that I've found this precious son, I'm going to do as much as I can to have him in my life as much as possible.

But I understand that Amanda is a huge part of his life too, and his time with her is limited now, due to her health. I couldn't imagine if my mom had cancer. She was in a car accident a while back and that was horrible. She just had a hurt leg from it. Things could have been so much worse.

We get to the house, and Hayden runs inside. Amanda is sitting at the table, eating something that looks like French toast, which I'm sure Lidia made for her. Hayden is talking a mile a minute, telling his mom all about Gordon the Ghoul and how Ronnie came and scared Jenni.

"But I wasn't scared at all! I thought Ronnie was a bear at first. I was a little scared then, but when he started laughing, I stopped feeling afraid."

"That sounds like Ronnie," Amanda says. "I saw him again last night. He was asking where you guys had gone because he wanted to see Hayden, but by then it was too late for him to join you all."

I can't help but wonder if Ronnie still has feelings for Amanda.

"Well, he did see him a little bit last night, but it was so dark, it wasn't much of a meeting," I say.

Jenni is still withdrawn, and we haven't really gotten a chance to speak since our conversation last night. She loads her plate with Lidia's French toast and then takes a seat at the table near Amanda. I grab my own plate of food and then join them.

"I'd like Hayden to be able to meet his uncles," I say. "We have a big race in a couple of weeks. I'd like to bring Hayden to it so he can meet them."

Mom comes into the room. "Your dad just called. He will be in town tonight, so Hayden can meet him first thing in the morning."

"What about Kaison and Ariana?" Last I'd heard, they were on a trip to the Maldives.

"They'll both be at the big race," Mom says. "Ashton won't be in town. He's been dealing with that merger in Singapore. But maybe we could do a video call, and you can have Hayden meet him."

"What about Brensen? Is he still in Africa?"

"Yes, but if you reach out to him, he might come back home on the plane he keeps there." Our family has multiple private jets since we're traveling around the country so often. It makes it much easier to get around since we don't have to deal with finding plane tickets.

I shoot him a text with a picture of me and Hayden that we took the day we bought the cowboy hats. Brensen texts back.

I'd heard you had a secret kid. It's crazy how much he looks like you.

I'm guessing Mom told you. Sorry I haven't reached out yet. I've been a little overwhelmed with the whole fatherhood thing.

No worries at all.

I invite him to come back for the race in a couple of weeks, and he agrees to make the arrangements for travel.

For the siblings who haven't met Hayden yet, I send the picture in our family group chat and get a variety of responses with people saying they want to meet him.

Then we jump on a video call with everyone in the family and I show Hayden off to them. Callie and Weston are so excited they decide to pack up Angel and come over.

When Callie and Weston show up, Angel is toddling around Hayden, and it's sweet to see his face light up when she approaches him.

"We have an announcement to make," Weston says with a big grin.

Callie places a hand on her belly. "Weston and I are expecting our first child." Since Angel was from her first marriage, this is the first baby she's having with Weston. Although, he's stuck around for Angel's entire life and was there for most of the pregnancy, even if he didn't know about it at first.

"That's great news," Jenni says. "Congratulations."

I can tell she's putting on a brave face, but I can't imagine what she's feeling inside, knowing she'll never be able to carry her own baby inside her.

They pull out the ultrasound pictures, and my mom is in grandmother heaven, oohing and ahhing.

"I should probably go home. I need a shower anyway. I smell like campfire," Jenni says to me and begins to walk away. But her voice is off, and I can only imagine the pain she's going through seeing Callie and Weston announcing their first child. Jenni isn't the type to make a big deal about it or make it about her, but that doesn't mean she's not hurting either.

I catch up to her by the front door. "Hey, are you okay?"

Her gaze flits to the living room. "You're missing out on the fun."

"They'll still be there in five minutes." My heart is twisting in knots at Jenni's confession last night and now this? "I know this must be hard for you."

"I just need to go, Langston. It's not something you can fix."

"What about us?"

Jenni breathes out a heavy sigh. "I don't think it's a good idea to continue this relationship."

She might as well have punched me in the gut. Hard. "You can't be serious."

"I am. I've thought about it most of the night. I could hardly sleep after our conversation."

"And you've decided what we're feeling isn't worth fighting for?" The old pain of abandonment flares up again, and it's hard to breathe. "Am I the only one feeling this?" I wave a hand between us. Desperation rises in my voice.

She bites her lip, and her gaze slides away from me.

"Don't lie to me, Jenni."

"I want to be with you more than anything. But I can't put you through the pain that being with me would inflict on you."

Those were the words I was hoping she wouldn't say. And I can't think of a single thing to say to change her mind.

"Goodbye, Langston. You might as well tell your family we're broken up, because I can't handle the fake romance anymore. It's too hard."

And without another word, she walks out the door. I've never felt so helpless in my entire life.

"Is everything okay?" Mom comes up to me. Her mom radar must have been going off because nothing is okay. I fall into her arms, and she squeezes me and pats me on the back. I'm grateful that Hayden can't see me from where he is in the living room, thanks to the fireplace that sections off the living room from the grand entrance.

"She just left," I choke out.

"Honey, I'm sure she'll be back. She just lives across town."

"No, she left me. Ended things," I clarify.

"What? What happened?"

Another relationship destroyed, another woman walking out on me. It's like I'm cursed.

"What's wrong with me, Mom? Why do I chase off all the women in my life?"

She pulls back and looks at me, her eyes full of concern. "I don't know what's going on with you and that girl, but there is nothing wrong with you, my precious boy."

I want to leave, go home, and zone out in front of the TV, but I have a kid in the other room who is meeting his cousin for the very first time. I don't want to miss it, and now I'm regretting my decision to corner Jenni when she was trying to leave. My heart aches so much with the loss. I want to chase after Jenni, try to talk sense into her, but I need to let her have the space she seems to want.

I fight my hardest to pull myself together, and I go back into the living room where Hayden and Amanda are talking to my brother and his wife and adopted child.

Angel is sitting on the floor next to a basket of blocks, and Hayden is crouched on the ground building a tower. Angel smacks it down and then starts clapping.

"We play this game a lot at home," Callie says.

"Want to do another one?" Hayden asks in a sweet voice to Angel.

"I'm not close to my siblings anymore," Amanda says, "so Hayden hasn't had the chance to play with his other cousins. But he's really good with her."

I can't help but wonder if Amanda is beginning to regret her decision to keep Hayden away from us all this time.

Hayden builds another block tower, and Angel knocks it down, giggling hysterically. Her soft, dark hair is pulled up into a little ponytail with an over-sized pink bow. Callie always has her dressed in the cutest little outfits, and I have no doubt my mom has a hand in that. She loves to spoil her little grand-daughter.

It's scenes like these that make Jenni think she can't be with me. It hurts that she can't trust me enough to let me decide if I'm okay with not having more kids one day. And now she's leaving me just like Sarah and Amanda.

It's not that I still want either one of them, but I'm clearly not over the feeling of abandonment that they left me with. It hurts to be left, and in Amanda's case, there wasn't even an explanation given. To this day, I still don't know what I did to cause her to leave. Am I that bad at being a husband that I can't hold a marriage together?

"Where did Jenni go?" Weston asks.

"She went home," I say.

He looks over at me, taking in my expression. "Hey, man. Are you okay?"

I shake my head slightly.

"Come here." He stands and gestures toward the

conference room. Mom looks over at me and watches as we leave, and I can only assume that she's glad Weston is there for me.

Weston pulls the door shut when we get to the conference room. "What's going on?"

"Jenni and I broke up."

His brows knit together in concern. "Oh, no. I thought you guys were so happy together. What happened?"

"I can't go into too much detail because I want to protect Jenni's privacy. But she ended things with me today."

"I'm sorry to hear that. And I don't mean to pry. I just want to make sure you're okay."

"She's not the problem at all. I don't want you to think she did anything wrong. It's just... complicated." Because Jenni is wonderful in so many ways. "If anything, she's being noble. Too noble, if you ask me."

"You can't control what others do. We all have to learn that the hard way, don't we?" Weston says.

"Jenni has to figure out things for herself, but the situation is just really hard and sad. That's all I can really say." My heart aches so much when I think of Jenni. But I love her, and that love has only grown seeing how she's trying to protect me, as frustrating as that may seem.

"What I've had to learn from my own experience

being married is that you have to have so much compassion and patience for the other person."

"I wonder if part of our problem is that we moved too quickly," I say.

"I don't know if that's true. You and Jenni have been brewing some chemistry for quite a while. We've all seen it from a distance. I think these feelings were there, but neither of you were acknowledging them. By the way, how's Ronnie feeling about all of this?"

"He's not happy. He thinks I should stay away from Jenni. Well, he's getting his wish granted now. She doesn't want to be with me," I say miserably.

"This girl has you all sorts of torn up," Weston says. "I know the feeling. Callie had me the same way." He shakes his head with a smile. "I hope you two work it out. I'm rooting for you two, and I know all the family feels the same way."

"Thanks, but I don't see how this could be worked out. Jenni seems to have her mind made up."

"Don't give up hope. You never know what could happen." He grins at me. "Who knows, maybe this time next year the two of you will be announcing your own little one on the way."

I groan inwardly and give him a stiff smile.

Weston looks at me hesitantly. "Did I say something wrong? You're giving me a funny look."

I shake my head. "It's nothing." The truth is, there's nothing more that I'd like than to hold Jenni's baby in my arms. There's got to be more that can be done to help her have kids if she wants them so badly. Maybe in vitro or a surrogate. I don't know much about infertility, but I'm not willing to give up hope. And she can still have a foster child if she wants. I just want her, and I want her to be happy. More than anything. It's destroying me to know that she's been in all this pain and has been hiding it all this time.

I'm just learning about this fight, and I don't want to give up so easily. Is that insensitive of me?

"Hey, whatever you two are going through, I hope you know I'm here for you both. Jenni is already like family to me. I'd love for her to become my sister-in-law one day."

"I'd like that too. I know I'm in love with her. I think I have been for quite some time and haven't been willing to admit it to myself."

"She's a fiery one and was keeping you at arm's length. I wonder if it had to do with the way she was feeling too," Weston says.

"I don't know. But I am worried about her. I hate to think that she's home alone and suffering. I feel so helpless. I want to go after her, but I also think she might need some space."

"I know you'll figure out what the right thing to do is."

"Weston?"

"Yeah?"

"Do you think there's something wrong with me? Some reason why I might be chasing off the women in my life?" I hate feeling this vulnerable in front of my brother. It's not like me. Usually, we're all bravado and macho.

"Well, your ears are kind of funny shaped."

I slap a hand to my ears. "You have the same funny shaped ears."

He only laughs at me. "You asked me, and that's my answer. Also, you could use a little mouthwash. Your breath is pretty bad."

"I just brushed my teeth at the campground this morning. And I used mouthwash. You think I wanted to be stinky around Jenni?" That's what I get for asking Weston for his honest opinion.

"All kidding aside, there's nothing wrong with you, bro. You're a Keith. We're all handsome devils. We work hard, and we love even harder. We're loyal and family means everything to us. If there are women out there who don't want a piece of that, then it's their issue, not yours. Now, that doesn't mean you can't improve a little. Like brushing your teeth more."

The punk. I have excellent hygiene. I cover my mouth and breathe into my hand. Now he's making me paranoid. No bad smells, but I pop in a mint just to cover my bases.

Weston slaps me on the back in a brotherly way. "Should we get back out there? There's some overwhelming cuteness on display between those two kiddos out there."

I follow him to the living room where Hayden is playing peek-a-boo with Angel by hiding behind the couch and then popping up to make her dissolve into the cutest giggles.

My heart swells to see my son being so good with his little cousin, and I'm proud to call him my own.

15

JENNI

I go home and shower, but the hot water does nothing to relax me. Langston's devastated face is all I can see and think about and it's tearing my heart out. I scrub at my hair with a vengeance, but it's not helping me get my frustration out. I feel like screaming. Why did this have to happen to me? If it weren't for this infertility, Langston and I would probably be together and happy right now.

And how I wish I could feel his arms around me. I need his comforting arms, but I can't have them. I can't hurt him like this. Hot tears run down my face and mingle with the water falling on me.

After my shower is finished, I turn off the water and let the sobs fully loose as I climb from the shower and wrap a towel around me. Because now I haven't just lost my ability to bear my own children. Now I've lost Langston, and there's no way to make it better. It's hitting me now how deeply I care for him, how deeply I've cared for such a long time.

He's always been there, even when we were "enemies" or whatever you want to call it. I've been lying to myself about him for a long time, and now that I've finally admitted my feelings for him, I've lost him. Not just as a boyfriend, but as a friend too. I don't hang out with a lot of girls. I never really have. It's always been me and Ronnie and the Keith boys, mostly Langston.

How can I even face his family now? They're going to have so many questions about why we're breaking up. And Langston won't have answers for them, not unless he's willing to tell my secret, which I know he would never do. So he's just stuck in this weird place where he can't explain the breakup to anyone.

But I know he'll be better off in the end. He's an amazing catch. He can find a woman who can give him the babies he deserves. That will never be me. I've known I was playing with fire, but I got caught up in the moment and allowed myself to fall in love.

Maybe it's just better if I never get married. I'll just have my foster kids, eventually adopt some babies. Some people don't get their happy-ever-afters, and that's just life.

Noodle meows, coming up to me as I'm getting dressed. I sit on my bed, scrolling through pictures of Langston and me at the theater, and Noodle curls up next to me, like she understands how sad I am. She's always been like that. She's a fantastic emotional support animal, even though I didn't get her for that reason. She purrs and stays with me as I allow myself to have a good cry. I just sit there and pet her and pet her, and she never moves away.

Once I'm dressed and my hair is dried, a knock sounds on my front door. I go get it to find my mom on my doorstep.

"What is wrong with you, Jenni?" She comes in and stares at my face, which I'm sure is puffy from all the crying I've been doing.

I don't know where to start. The tears are fighting to fall again. I've always been the strong one who holds everything inside. And now that I've lost Langston, the floodgates are open.

My mom doesn't seem to accept the fact that I'm not answering her question, so she fires another one at me. "What's this I hear about you breaking up with Langston? Tell me it's not true, and that this is just some little spat you've had."

So she's been talking to Laurie again. Big surprise.

"It's true," I choke out.

I can't see through my tears, but then my mom's arms are around me, and she's patting me on the back. "There must be some way we can fix this, my dear girl."

"There's not. This time, everything is broken beyond repair."

"That can't be true." She pulls back and strokes my hair back from my face, looking into my eyes. She's blurry through my tears. "I've never seen you cry like this. What has gotten into you?"

"Mom, I'm not the daughter you think I am."

"Nonsense, you're still my little Jenni. Nothing you could do or say would change that."

"I can't give you the life you've always wanted as the proud grandma," I choke out.

"You may not have been able to work things out with Langston, but there are other men. My sister has one already picked out for you in India. He's a wonderful man. His father owns a very large hotel chain. All the best of the best resorts in Asia."

"Mom!" I exclaim. "I don't want to date a guy from India. I want Langston. I'm in love with him. I can't even think about dating someone else right now."

"Then what's the problem? Laurie says you've broken his heart. Go over there and make it better. There's still time to repair things."

I don't know how to get through to her that this isn't going to work out the way she thinks. "No, Mom. It won't be better. Langston and I can never be together."

"You're overreacting. You just wait. You'll be popping out his babies before long." She gets this dreamy look in her eyes, and I can't take another minute of this.

"I will never pop out any babies. That's what I've been trying to tell you."

"You just need to be a bit more optimistic."

"Optimism isn't going to help me. I'm infertile." There. I've finally said it.

My mom's mouth falls open. "What are you talking about?"

"The doctor confirmed it. I can't bear children."

"No. That can't be true." She sits frozen for a second, like she can't find the right words to say.

"It's true."

"My dear girl." She pulls me to her and instead of being upset and crying, she just holds me. She pulls away and looks at me. "How long have you known this?"

"For about a year."

"And you've just carried this news around with you, never telling us or allowing us to help you through it?" Her eyes widen in realization. "All those times I told you I wanted you to get married and have babies... You never said anything." She looks horrified. "What you must have been feeling..." She shakes her head. "I wish you could have felt comfortable enough to tell us the truth. We only want to love you and support you."

My heart warms at her words. "I never wanted you to feel this pain I was feeling. I knew how disappointed you'd be. Being a grandmother is all you can talk about these days."

"And maybe that day will come. You can still adopt."

"Yes, I know. I've already been thinking about becoming a foster mom. I was going to tell you soon. But I knew it would be a tough conversation, so I was putting it off. Now I wish I'd been brave enough to tell you sooner."

"So is this why you broke up with Langston?" my mom asks.

I nod, wiping away the last of the tears that have recently fallen. I'm a complete mess. At least I haven't put on any makeup yet. I'd look like a raccoon if I had.

She looks furious for a minute. "Did that boy tell you he didn't want to be with you because you couldn't have his babies?"

"No, Mom. Of course not. You should know Langston better than that." But truthfully, I don't really know what Langston thinks about my infertility. Not fully. We've only talked about it briefly.

"Then why aren't you with him? None of this is making any sense."

"I can't be the one to keep him from bearing children. Not when I know now that I'm the messed up one."

"You are perfect as you are. This is only a trial you

are facing in this life. If Langston truly loves you, he will marry you regardless."

"That's what I'm afraid of. I've seen the way his mom talks about the day she has more grandchildren. It would break her heart if she knew she wouldn't have Langston's children toddling around her house."

"She has Hayden, and don't forget that she has many other sons who can have babies. You're thinking too negatively and sacrificing yourself for no good reason."

"You think so?" I ask.

"Yes, definitely. I think you ought to talk to Laurie about it and let her put in her opinion. Why decide for her? That woman adores you and would be thrilled to have you as her daughter-in-law, even if you never bear children with Langston's DNA."

"I've never really thought about talking to Laurie about it."

Mom picks up her phone. "We can call her now. I bet you she'd come over right away. She's concerned for her son."

"I don't know, Mom." I wipe at my eyes. "I think I'm going to need a bit more time to process all of this."

She covers my hand with hers. "I understand."

J drive down to Gainesville for an informational meeting on becoming a foster parent. The process is supposed to take about six months or so, but I leave the meeting more excited than ever. I really could make a difference in a child's life. Even if I were to be able to have children, I think I'd want to do this. More than anything, I want to help these dear children. There are so many households out there that can't provide good lives for these children.

I stop by a fast-food place and grab a burger and a large Diet Coke. I don't usually eat fast food, but I'm in the mood for it now. There's something about eating greasy fries and a juicy hamburger that makes me feel a little better about life.

I keep imagining a little girl or little boy walking into my home for the first time, seeing where they're going to live. I'd have to get a nanny for them while I'm at work, and I'd want the best. I'd be happy with a child of any age, honestly.

Sipping on my soda, I pull up to the stoplight next to Hayden's school just as classes are letting out. He was supposed to have just had his first day of school yesterday. I've been so detached from what's been going on with him. And now I feel horrible because I've become this person in his life that he's started to get attached to and I've just ghosted him.

Would Langston be okay with me coming to see

Hayden? Would that be too hard? To be around Langston as a friend again? It's not like I can just avoid him. He's too big a part of my life.

I see Hayden running out to his mom's car. He stops and sees me at the corner and waves with a giant smile on his face, and I wonder if he knows Langston and I have broken up.

I wave back. From what I've heard from my mom, Amanda has found a place of her own, and they've just moved in.

I head home, and Noodle greets me at the door with a meow. She's been up to no good while I've been gone.

"What have you done, sweet kitty?" There are noodles strung all over the living room like she's been rolling in it. There's one noodle hanging down from the end table, and she runs around the house like a wild animal before attacking it.

Where did all this pasta come from anyway? I go into the kitchen to see that I'd forgotten to put my leftovers away last night from when I went out to eat and the clamshell lid has a giant hole bitten into the top of it. So much for that pesto. Apparently, Noodle thinks they're the best toys ever. Why do I even bother with the giant kitty condo I have for her downstairs? I just need to get her a room full of noodles that she can roll around in.

My doorbell rings, and I open it to discover that

Langston is standing on my front porch. My heart goes into panic mode. He looks good, like he's just gotten a haircut, and his beard is neatly trimmed. He's wearing a shirt I've never seen before, and he's holding a black bundle.

"Hi," is all I can say.

"Can I come in?" he asks.

"Um, sure." I open the door wider so he can pass me, and when he does, I catch a whiff of his cologne, which is a mixture of pine and warm spices.

"I brought over your hoodie. You forgot it at my mom's house." He hands the black bundle to me.

"Oh thanks. I was wondering where that went." My heart is racing faster than Valentine, and I ache for this man. "How are things with Amanda?"

"She's all moved into her new place, but Hayden is having a hard time adjusting to his new school. There was a bully who picked on him the first day there for being a bratty rich kid. Amanda isn't happy about it. I hope she doesn't regret her decision to bring him here and take him back." His face is pale as he talks about it, and I can sense a bit of the worry he's facing.

"Hey, you know about him now. She can't just take him away from you anymore."

His shoulders relax a bit at my words. "That's true. I've called my lawyer, and I'm going to take the paternity test tomorrow. There's no doubt Hayden is my son, but I need the official papers that prove that he is. Who knows, Amanda might get well and decide to run away with Hayden at any time. She spooks easily, as we all well know."

"Anything could happen," I agree. "You're smart to cover your bases."

We head into the living room and sit on my white couches. These will probably be trashed one day by my future foster kids, but I don't even care. I'll get them professionally cleaned or something.

Langston doesn't even know how far I've gotten in the process. We haven't talked at all since we broke up.

His gaze collides with mine. "I miss you. Maybe we won't be together long term, but I still want to spend time with you."

"I don't think that's a good idea." It's too hard to be around him and not have him, allow him to put his arms around me, to kiss me. My heart can hardly take being around him now.

"Our families are best friends. You're not going to be able to cut me out of your life completely. You know that, right?"

I sigh. "I know. But it doesn't have to mean you're coming over here and sitting alone with me either."

"I understand. I'm sorry if I made you uncomfortable." He gets up. "I'll give you the space you want." He walks to the door and stops to turn. "Hayden misses you."

I press my lips together because if I speak, I'm

going to fall into his arms and ask him to ignore everything I've just said. I want to joke around with him, laugh like we used to or talk smack to each other. But the old Jenni and Langston don't exist anymore. We've been replaced by these two heartbroken people who can barely hold a conversation without feeling some amount of pain. And in this case, it's a huge amount of pain, on my part anyway. And if the look on Langston's face is a reflection of the misery he's feeling, then I'd say he's pretty bad off himself.

Finally, I gather some words together. "I miss Hayden too. Tell him I said hi and that I'll see him at the Blue Mountain Derby."

"I'll tell him." Langston doesn't tease me about winning, and now I wish he would. At this point I'd be happy to let Thunder win if it meant I could fix our situation. And that's saying a lot.

16

LANGSTON

When Wednesday rolls around, it's my turn to take Hayden. It's the first time he's sleeping at my house, and I have his room all set up, thanks to some help from my personal assistant, Maggie. She's an older woman, but very tech savvy, which is important for me since I'm a techie myself. She did a bunch of online shopping for me and decorated his room in a palette of blues, which she discovered is his favorite color. She's a mother and grandmother and knows a lot about what kids like. I'm clueless, so I'm grateful for her help. Mom has been a huge help too, going out with Maggie to buy clothes for Hayden.

I pull up to his school, and he's in a pretty ratty looking t-shirt and jeans. Didn't Amanda want to put him in some of the new clothes we bought for him?

He climbs into the car, and he's using his old beat-up backpack instead of the brand new one Maggie picked out. We'd sent them over to Amanda's new place, but for whatever reason, she's not letting him use the items.

"Where's that new backpack we got you?" I ask.

"Oh, Mom donated it to the thrift store. She said the backpack I have is just fine."

I clench my fists, but don't want to make a big deal in front of Hayden, so I say, "Do you want a new backpack?"

He juts out his bottom lip. "Yeah. I really liked that one. It had dinosaurs on it, and the one Mom makes me wear is red and ugly. I hate red."

Duly noted. Don't get the kid anything red. Stick to blues. "How about green?"

He shrugs. "Green's okay."

I glance in the rear-view mirror, and he's not buckled up. He's staring out the window.

"Put on your seatbelt, buddy. The lady behind me looks impatient." She looks like the typical soccer mom with pickup line road rage, messy bun and all. I only know about this from my mom's social media feed that's filled with various moms and grandmas helping to pick up kids.

In the future, I'll have to get a nanny to pick up Hayden from school. I've already started the process of searching for one. I have so many meetings in Atlanta for the company. I don't take as many trips overseas as my brothers do, so that makes it easier to be there for Hayden. But there will definitely be days where I won't be around as much as I'd like. But that's something any single parent has to deal with.

A big redheaded kid passes by my car as I'm pulling out and makes an intimidating face at Hayden.

Hayden sighs and buckles up. "Dad, no one likes me at school. I hate being the new kid."

"Who was that boy just now?" I refrain from opening the door and giving him a piece of my mind. That would probably only make it worse for Hayden.

"That was Christopher Walker. The biggest bully at school."

"That's the kid who's been mean to you?"

"Yeah, ever since my first day."

"Did you say his last name was Walker?" The Walkers have never liked our family. They call us snooty and uppity and have been aggressive at the local bar toward us on more than one occasion.

"Yeah. He stole my lunch and ate it himself, and my mom made me peanut butter and jelly, my favorite."

"Did you get anything to eat?"

"No." He's on the verge of tears. "I'm starving. I tried to tell my teacher, but she wouldn't listen."

"Well, as soon as we get you home, we'll get you some food. Would that help?"

Hayden sniffles. "Yeah."

"I'm sorry." And this is one of the reasons I don't want Hayden to go to the regular elementary school. If he were tutored, he wouldn't have to face this kind of bullying. And he's only being bullied because he's a Keith. He may have a different last name, thanks to Amanda never allowing him to take mine, but it's no secret that Hayden has moved to Blue Mountain because he's my long-lost son. People in this small town gobble up a story like that faster than a starving teenager at a pizza place.

I kind of feel like cornering the kid's dad and telling him to keep his son in line, but I doubt that would do any good. I'm not going to go all mafia on the dude. It's not really my style.

But that doesn't mean I'm going to do nothing either. "I'll talk to your mom, and we can tell the school. He's not going to get away with this."

"Okay." His little voice sounds so scared and over-whelmed. If I weren't driving, I'd take him in my arms and help make it all better. But I'm not sure how he'd feel about it. It's bad enough that he's moving into not only a new home with his mom, but now he's moving into my house too.

It's going to be a lot for him to handle at once, and I'm terrified I won't be able to know the right ways to help. Maybe Jenni is right, and we do need that family therapy. I'll have to get Maggie to look into it.

We pull up to the house, and it hits me that this is a

start of a new era. I'm officially on my own as a dad. Before this, I had Mom, Jenni, and Amanda stepping in to help.

Just thinking about Jenni causes a heavy ache to build within me. I've barely heard from her. How am I going to face fatherhood without her by my side? She's so good with Hayden. The irony of this situation is that she doesn't want to be with me because we couldn't have kids. But I already have one right in front of me, and I'm desperate for her help.

Hayden climbs out of the car when I've parked it in the garage, and he heads into the house.

"Want to see your new room?" I ask, following him.

"Sure." That seems to cheer him up a bit. He dashes toward it. I showed him last week which room it would be. It used to be my guest room, but we've redecorated it and brought in toys, a new tablet for him —set up with parental controls at Maggie's insistence —and a plethora of new stuffed animals. Maggie insisted those would help to comfort him when he misses his mom.

"Do you have any favorite toys you want over here from your mom's?"

"Yeah, but she won't let me bring any of them over here." His face is sullen.

"Why not?" I ask.

"She says it's best if we keep our households separate."

That would probably explain why she decided to give away the backpack. And who knows what else?

"Okay. The good news is, we have some pretty great stuffed animals here. Miss Maggie picked them out for you."

He grabs a squishy stuffed whale and wraps his arms around it. "I'm going to name this one Wilbur the Whale." He climbs up onto his bed and sets Wilbur next to him. "What's this?" He picks up the tablet.

I show him how to work it, and before long, his worries are forgotten as he starts downloading various learning apps and games.

I'd have to give Maggie a raise after all the wonderful things she's thought of.

"There are limits to how many hours a day you can use the tablet. It turns off right before bedtime too, so don't think about staying up late sneaking it into bed with you."

Maggie had warned me that this might be a problem since her grandkids do that a lot.

"Are you hungry? Stella bought us a bunch of snacks. Kid ones too. You like goldfish and superhero fruit snacks?"

"Yeah!" He jumps off the bed and races toward the kitchen.

My pantry is stocked with little juice boxes, macaroni and cheese, and a variety pack of chips. I grab out the ones I promised and get Hayden settled at the table with them. "If you're still hungry, I can make you a corn dog, but dinner will be soon, so I don't want to spoil your appetite too much."

"You won't spoil my appetite, I promise." Hayden rips open his goldfish package and starts eating. "I can eat a lot."

Sausage waddles into the room and wags his tail at Hayden. The two of them got acquainted the first day Hayden came to visit my house right after he arrived. Sausage plants his rear right next to Hayden's chair and pants.

"Gross, Sausage. Your breath is horrible."

"Come on, boy. Leave Hayden alone." I shoo him away and head to the microwave when it beeps with Hayden's cooked corn dog.

When I bring the plate over to Hayden, Sausage is right by his side again. "Whatever. I give up. You win, pooch." I swear I'm the biggest pushover when it comes to this dog.

I go grab myself a bag of corn chips from the pantry. Who knew having a kid around would mean my house would be stocked up with the good snacks? Maggie insisted on it. She said it was important for him to feel welcome, and that food was a good way for him to feel at home. I guess the saying "the way to a man's heart is through his stomach" works on little men too. Hayden is happily chowing down.

"I never eat chips like this." Usually, I'm eating

something healthy like dried mangos specially ordered or organic nuts with dried berries. This is a nice change of pace. I guess Maggie figured Hayden wouldn't be into the dried fruit and nuts I usually eat. But now that I'm eating these chips, I realize I'm not so into it anymore either.

I glance over to see Hayden reaching down to hand a chunk of corn dog to Sausage, but instead of taking the chunk offered, Sausage takes the entire thing, stick and all, and races away with it to his favorite eating corner. I don't know why, but he has to eat all his food secretly and in the same spot behind my recliner.

He finishes off the corn dog and starts chewing up the stick.

"Hey, enough of that, you crazy dog." I come over to where he is, and he looks up at me with sheepish eyes. "You know you were being naughty. Now I'm going to have to get Hayden another corn dog."

"It's okay, Dad. You don't have to get me another one."

"Hayden?" I sit next to him. "Why did you decided to call me Dad when you first met me?"

"Why wouldn't I? You're my dad."

"But I haven't been around."

"I know. But I always knew you would be the great-est. And I was right."

This kid is melting my heart. How will I ever be

able to discipline him? I'm going to be too busy spoiling him rotten.

"I think you're pretty great too."

"I just wish I could have met you sooner. I would have liked to have a dad before."

"Me too." My heart is heavy, thinking about the years we'd lost. Hayden's had to grow up pretty quickly in the past few weeks. He seems much older than a kid his age.

A horrible smell permeates the air.

"Ew, Dad, did you pass gas?"

I laugh. "It wasn't me. I swear."

He looks down, and sure enough Sausage is sitting there, wagging his tail like he's proud of himself. "Gross. I bet it was Sausage."

"He's just one of the guys," I say. "No shame. He just lets it rip."

"I bet you don't do that around Jenni," Hayden says with a big, silly smile.

"I sure don't." My face grows warm as a memory comes to mind. "Okay, it did happen once. We were on her family's yacht."

"What's a yacht?"

"It's a big fancy boat. I'll take you out on it sometime. But back to the story. We were out on this yacht, and Jenni and I had eaten way too many bean burritos. She wanted to play board games, and we got into this big competitive game of Risk. I was about to win, but then my belly started cramping up from all the beans I'd eaten, and I kept trying to hold it inside. But then I sat a little funny to the side, and it just slipped out. It stunk so bad. I was so embarrassed because even back then I had a little bit of a crush on Jenni."

Hayden bursts into giggles. "Did she know it was you?"

"I don't think so. I completely denied it, and since no one would fess up, I was off the hook."

"Did you win the game?" Hayden asks.

"I couldn't tell you. All I can remember is that terrible fart."

Hayden gets a kick out of this. "I would be so embarrassed. At my old school, there was this girl named Emily that I liked, and I let one out in front of her. It was loud, and she looked right at me. It was really embarrassing." His face has gone red just talking about it.

It's nice sitting here with Hayden, laughing and joking. And I can't believe he's even opening up to me about his crush. "I wanted a dad for so long. This is completely awesome."

I didn't even know I had a son, but I agree. It's incredible, and we have so much time ahead of us to bond even more.

I just wish Jenni were here to experience it with us.

~

*a*fter dropping Hayden off at school the next morning, I head to Blue Mountain Brewery to grab my favorite coffee. I take it black, and their specialty coffee is really good here.

I won't always be able to drop Hayden off, but this first week of bonding is important so I'm taking the extra time away from work to spend as much time with him as possible.

When I step inside the cozy coffee shop, a bunch of my mom's knitting club friends are all sitting around talking.

Joyce Gregory and Maybelline Richardson look up and wave when they see me. Joyce's gray hair is frizzed out all around her shoulders, and her glasses look like they're swallowing her face whole. Maybelline has short red curls surrounding her rounded face.

"Hello there, Langston," Maybelline calls when I've gotten my coffee.

"Hello, Miss Maybelline." I nod to the rest of the group. "Ladies."

"Come sit down. We have an extra chair." Joyce waves me over.

"I, uh." I can't think of a reason not to. "Well, okay. For a little bit then." They've known me since I was born, so I can't really deny them anything.

"What's this I hear about you breaking up with Jenni Finley?" Maybelline chides.

"Well, I didn't even know they were dating," Olive Leslie says. She has a halo of teased up white-blonde hair surrounding her head like an angel.

"Where have you been?" Maybelline says. "They're the hottest item Blue Mountain has ever seen—well, at least they were before they broke up. Both of them locals. You don't see that too often. Most of the kids around here marry someone from the big city."

"You sound like you've been talking to my mom," I say.

"Oh, yes, dear. She keeps us well informed," Joyce says, bringing her coffee cup to her lips. "Although Olive hasn't been paying attention," she adds before taking a sip.

"I've been traveling. Florida is so nice this time of year. I'm behind on all the news."

"We were all rooting for you," Maybelline says.

"You poor dear," Joyce says. "You must be so devastated. Jenni is quite the catch."

"I am," I say honestly. "Jenni is the best of the best."

"Then surely there's something you can do to make it better," Maybelline says. "If you want to, that is. This does seem to be a delicate situation."

"What do you mean by that?" Joyce asks. "Do you know the reason they broke up? No one can seem to figure it out."

Maybelline leans forward like she has the juiciest gossip of all. "Well, it seems that poor Jenni can't ever get pregnant and doesn't want to burden Langston into a childless marriage."

What? Jenni finally told her mom she can't have kids? What could have possibly led her to do that?

I open my mouth to speak, but then Joyce pipes up before I can. "Where did you hear this?"

Jenni would be so upset if she heard her privacy being violated like this.

"I overheard Meera pouring her heart out to Eliza Harvey at the diner yesterday."

Eliza Harvey, the wife of the owner of the diner, is one of Meera's closest friends, so it makes sense that she would have confided in her. After all, the poor woman must have been hurting herself, and knowing Meera, she never would have wanted Jenni's secret to be spread around like this.

I speak up. "I'm not sure Jenni would appreciate this being so openly discussed."

They whip their heads back to where I am like they've almost forgotten I was there. "Oh, dear," Maybelline says. "Langston, you have to forgive us. We're just so concerned about the two of you. I didn't mean to overstep." Her eyes are genuinely sorrowful, and she places her hand over mine. "We're here for you both if you ever need anything."

"Thank you. I appreciate that." At least she does seem to be remorseful.

I leave the coffee shop and get into my car. Jenni

deserves to know her secret is being spread around town, and I want it to come from me, not one of the town gossips. I pick up my phone and give her a call.

"Langston?"

It's good to hear her voice. I want to bask in it for a moment, but I need to get to the point too. "Hey, Jenni. I need to talk to you about something unpleasant."

"Okay?" A bit of nervousness has crept into her tone.

"I was just at the coffee shop, and the knitting club ladies all seem to know about your infertility."

"What? How?"

Hearing Jenni this upset makes me want to march right back in there and defend her some more. Those ladies are sweet and well meaning, but they are terrible about letting the rumors fly. They just can't keep secrets to themselves. "I'm guessing you told your mom about it?"

"Yes. Just barely."

"Well, Maybelline overheard your mom telling Eliza Harvey at the diner, and she just openly spoke about it to some of the knitting club members."

Jenni sighs. "That's so frustrating. But I guess they were going to figure it out eventually anyway. The main people I was hiding the news from were my parents, and now that they know, it doesn't really matter that the secret is out."

A weight lifts off my chest at her words. "That

makes sense. I was so worried that your privacy has been violated."

"I'm okay, Langston. I appreciate it, but I can handle the knitting club ladies. And my mom. I'm sure she's going through her own emotions and needs to talk it out with someone."

"I'm glad you were able to talk to your mom about it," I say.

Silence stretches between us.

"Yeah, it was good. I got to go. I have a work call coming in."

We end the call, and I lean back against my car's headrest and sigh. There's this little part of my heart that's hoping that if she was willing to talk to her mom, then maybe Meera was able to show her daughter that she's loved enough to deserve to have a husband who adores her regardless of whether she can have his babies or not.

A guy can dream, right?

17

JENNI

*J*ust as I'm finishing up work Friday night, my phone rings. I look down to see Valentine's trainer, Don Hopkins, is calling.

"Hey, Don. What can I do for you?"

"The vet came by today for Valentine's checkup." I was in a work meeting and had asked Don to handle the appointment for me.

"What did he say?" If Don is calling me about this, it can't be good.

"He's worried Valentine might be putting too much stress on his flexor tendon injury with all this heavy training we've been doing."

My stomach clenches. "Did he say he shouldn't race tomorrow?"

"He wasn't necessarily saying that, but it's something we need to watch out for. We just need to be cautious and ease up on the training some."

"The last thing I want is for Valentine to get hurt." As much as I don't want to, I might have to pull him from racing.

"I say we let him race this one, but if it doesn't go well, it may have to be his last."

"That's not the news I was hoping to hear tonight." Normally, I'd be freaking out that Langston might win the race, but at this point, does it even matter?

Maybe I'm being dramatic, but I'm falling deeper into depression these days, and the longer I go without Langston by my side, the worse it gets.

"What do you want to do? I recommend we try this one more race and see how it goes. If he performs fine, then we'll keep monitoring him, but I don't think he has much more in him. You may need to focus on another horse."

"Let's do it. If it's his last, then so be it. We can at least give it a good shot. Are you still over there?"

"Yes, ma'am."

"I'm going to head over to see how he's doing. I'll be there in ten minutes."

I send the email I was composing and grab a diet drink from my office mini fridge before heading out the door.

When I get to my parents' stables, Don goes into a bit more detail about how Valentine is doing, and we discuss options for other horses I can race next. Often racehorses don't get very many years racing, not more than three in many cases. It's so easy for them to get injured.

After we're finished talking, I head over to say hi to my mom. My dad is traveling at the moment, so she could probably use a little company. I let myself in through the back door.

"Hey, Mom, it's me," I call out.

"We're in here," she yells from the craft room. I head in there to find her surrounded by yarn and Laurie sitting across from her, both knitting up a storm.

"Oh, hi, Laurie."

"What brings you over here, sweetheart?" Laurie asks.

"I was just meeting with the trainer. The vet is concerned about Valentine's injury flaring up again after all the training I've been putting him through."

Laurie shakes her head. "These horses are always getting injured. Are you going to retire him then?"

"I may have to."

"What are you guys making?"

"I'm making a baby blanket for Weston and Callie's new little one," Laurie says.

"It's beautiful," I say, and my throat thickens to think of the sweet innocent baby being wrapped in it.

"I can't wait to hold their baby." If I can't have my

own, I'm at least going to snuggle all the babies I can get my hands on.

"Oh, honey, I heard that you're struggling."

"I'm not surprised. I heard the entire knitting club has been talking about my struggles. I wish you'd been a bit more discreet, Mom. Now I feel humiliated in front of the entire town."

"I'm sorry, Jenni." Mom's face is pale and distraught. "I never meant for this to spread like wildfire."

My shoulders slump. "I guess it doesn't matter now. There's nothing we can do to change what's happened."

"Maybe there's a silver lining to this incident," Mom says. "The town can rally around you now and support you. No one wishes you malice. And you've done nothing wrong. There's no need to feel humiliated."

"She's right," Laurie says. "And I'm so sorry." She sets her project down and gets up, coming over to where I'm standing and wrapping me in her arms.

The tension releases from my stiff spine at Laurie's embrace. I squeeze her back, and my heart fills with love. How can she take such an upsetting moment and turn it into something so sweet? I long to call her my mother-in-law. How many girls would be so lucky to have such a wonderful mother-in-law as she is? "Thank you. I needed a good Laurie hug."

"You can have one of these whenever you'd like." She pulls back and looks me in the eye. "And I mean it."

I wipe away a tear. I've been so stinking emotional lately. "Thank you." My voice is so croaky right now. You'd think it was my wedding day or something. All I'm doing is hugging Laurie.

"I do need you to think about something though."

"What's that?" I ask.

She looks at me sternly. "Giving Langston a chance. Go to him and make things right."

I shake my head. "I'm sorry. But I can't do that."

She puts her hands on her hips, all Southern and sassy. "Why ever not?"

"Because I can't be the reason that he doesn't have children of his own."

"He has Hayden."

"But," I protest, "he said he wants a whole house full of kids with me."

"Darlin', there are more ways than one to achieve that. You've punished yourself enough and deserve to be happy."

I sniffle. "You wouldn't feel sad that I wasn't having your flesh and blood?"

"Those babies are precious, and I'll love them as my own wherever they come from. They're all blessings from God. That's what matters. You've seen me with Callie's baby. You should know better than to think I wouldn't accept an adopted baby or a foster child as one of the bunch."

"And whatever you want to do," Mom says, "whether that's adopting or fostering, know that you're loved and valued just as you are. Your dad feels the same way."

"The Keiths are here to support you, too," Laurie says. "We'd love you as part of our family." She grins. "Not that I'm pressuring you or anything."

I can't help but laugh.

"But I wanted you to know that," Laurie continues. "We just want our Jenni to be okay."

"It feels like I'm running out of reasons to stay away from Langston."

"What's still stopping you?" Mom asks, clicking her knitting needles together.

"I don't know if Langston wants a woman who can't have his kids." It's hard to form the words. I feel bare and vulnerable.

"That's something you're going to have to work out with him," Laurie says. "I can't speak for him, but if you don't address this, you'll regret it for the rest of your life."

*L*aurie's words echo through my mind for the rest of the day. Normally, I'd be out doing something fun with Langston and Ronnie, but tonight Langston is with Hayden doing some father-son bonding.

I'm wallowing in my misery by eating a pint of ice cream. Usually, I eat the low-calorie kind, but tonight I went for the real stuff. Thick and creamy dark chocolate. I've been relying on food to help me through this. And diet drinks. And Noodle, who is faithfully curled up next to me purring as I watch a reality tv dating show that's on my large screen mounted on my bedroom wall. Langston had insisted I needed this TV, and he convinced me to buy it online. He's been working to get me to turn my house into a smart home, but I'm okay with flipping on switches the normal way.

My phone rings with a video call from Ronnie, and I swipe the screen. "Hey, don't mind the bedhead. I'm chilling tonight."

"Guess who I just talked to."

"I don't know... some new girl you're dating?" I toss out.

He makes a weird face. "Um, no. Why would you think that?"

"Because you're on the prowl?" I wave my ice-cream-laden spoon around to prove my point, but the frozen treat slides off it and lands onto my lap. "Eww." I grab a tissue from my bedside table and wipe the spot off my lap.

"Did you just spill ice cream on yourself?" Ronnie teases.

"Yes. Don't make fun of me."

"You really are pitiful. If you want Langston so bad, then why don't you just date him already?"

"Um, who are you and what have you done with my brother?" I throw the clump of tissue with the soggy glob of ice cream into the trash by my bed. It's filled with crumpled up cans of soda and dark chocolate wrappers. It's a good thing Ronnie is on the phone and not in person because he would definitely judge me right now.

"I just came home from Amanda's new place."

"You *what*?" I toss my spoon into my ice cream carton and set it on my bedside table.

"You heard me."

"What were you doing over there? That is literally the last place I would expect you to be."

"Why?"

"You know what? It kind of does make sense. You were into her back in the day, weren't you? That's what you and Langston are always fighting about. So did you put the moves on her? She is alone tonight since Hayden is over at Langston's. Did you kiss her or what?"

He laughs. "No, nothing like that. I was horribly rejected, in fact. But a man can try, can't he?"

"No offense, but that's a relief. You dating Amanda would be way too weird. Think of the custody situation Hayden would be in." I pause for a minute. "Wait a second. Why were you even trying that? Didn't you think of how messed up that would be?"

He shrugs. "When you like someone, you like them. People have done crazier things."

"Are you going to get yourself some ice cream now?"

He laughs. "Naw, I'm good. But I did want to talk to you about something."

"And that is?" I grab my ice cream again and settle in. This could go either way, good or bad, but whatever he's about to say is big. I can feel it in my bones.

"Amanda and I had a long talk about the past. She explained that she never knew I liked her back then, but even if she had, she wouldn't have been interested."

"Ouch!"

"I know. She said she just didn't feel a spark. Apparently, she still doesn't. And she's definitely not into rich men. Or dating, for that matter."

"The dating thing I can understand. She is sick, after all."

"Hey, sick people get into relationships all the time.

There are some good movies out there with that same plot," Ronnie says.

"But did you really want to get into a relationship with someone as sick as Amanda?"

"I mostly wanted closure. Answers. And I wanted to stop being angry with Langston. There was unfinished business to address."

"Does this mean you'll give your blessing if Langston and I get back together?" I dig around in the bottom of my ice cream container but then frown when I discover it's empty. No wonder I'm so bloated. That was probably as many calories as a meal at a fast-food place. And I've already eaten take out tonight.

"Are you saying you're considering it?" Ronnie seems surprised. "I thought you'd told him there was no way to fix it."

"I did tell him that."

"Well, if you think you might change your mind, you ought to let him know. He's all sorts of busted up over losing you."

"He is?"

"Oh yeah. The dude's a big mess. He's trying to hide it from Hayden, but even the kid is starting to catch on. And he misses you too."

"I know, Langston told me." Guilt sweeps through me. The last thing I want to do it hurt Hayden.

And I definitely don't want Langston to hurt either.

"Ronnie, I think I've made a big mistake. I thought I was doing him a favor, but now I'm realizing I'm not."

"How were you doing him a favor by breaking up with him? That sounds pretty backwards to me."

"I guess you haven't heard."

"No, I haven't. I know there's something going on with you, but no one has told me what that is. Supposedly, it's some huge secret."

"Not that huge. The knitting club all seems to know, so you might as well find out too."

"What? The kitting club knows and not me? Come on, sis. I'm your brother."

"I'm sorry, Ronnie. I should have told you. The truth is, I can't have kids."

Ronnie is dumbfounded. I can see it in his face.

"Wait. Really?"

"Yeah. There's nothing the doctor can do. My eggs are all dried up."

He makes a face. "Okay, TMI."

I laugh. "This is really sad, Ronnie."

"Oh." He looks sheepish. "Sorry. I really am. I'm just trying in my dumb way to make an awkward situation funny, and it's just... Just ignore me."

And this is why my brother doesn't have a girlfriend. Was that mean? It kind of was.

"But all joking aside, I hate to hear that, Jenni. You can't even do in vitro or anything, can you?"

I shake my head. "It's okay."

"Man, that's rough."

"I'm making my peace with it. I thought I had already, but then all these things have happened to make me realize that maybe keeping it a secret wasn't the greatest idea."

"No. I understand the need for privacy, but no one is going to judge you for that. It's not like you can help it. You haven't done anything wrong. And you're still the same Jenni we all love. Nothing will change that."

"You sound like Mom," I say.

"Well, she's a pretty smart lady, so I'll take that as a compliment."

"Ronnie?"

"Yeah?"

"Do you think Langston would ever want to marry me?"

"I think it's a little early to propose to him, sis. Maybe just start with dating for a while."

I laugh. "Okay. You're probably right about that. I know Langston really well, but a dating relationship is pretty different from a friendship."

"And not that long ago, it was a rivalry."

"Good point."

"Well, I've forgiven him for taking Amanda. I wish I'd just talked to her about it a long time ago. It would have saved me years of frustration."

"Maybe you ought to tell him next," I say.

"I think I'll do that." He stretches. "Have a good night, sis. See you at the race tomorrow."

"Bye." I end the call and set my phone down. My heart speeds up as I think about the possibility of Langston and me making things work.

My future might not be so grim after all.

18

LANGSTON

*T*he Blue Mountain race track is packed today, and Hayden is crazy excited for the derby to begin, chanting, "Go Thunder, go Thunder!" before the race even begins. We're both dressed appropriately with khaki pants and blazers atop collared shirts. Stella had everything ironed for us and hung up for us to wear.

We take our seats with the Finleys at our traditional owners' private box. We have caterers providing lunch before the game, and the family is slowly trickling in.

I've spent every spare moment either with Hayden or with the trainer trying to get Thunder ready for this race. Hayden has loved it and is just as excited as I am for the race. The only thing putting a damper on this day is that Jenni doesn't want to share it with me.

I've worked hard to give her the space she seems to want, and it's been tough. Working with the trainer has been a welcome distraction, and I've kind of thrown myself into it to keep my mind off of what's been going on with Jenni.

But there's no avoiding her today. She's here wearing a blue dress and matching hat propped on the side of her head with a large blue bow, and she looks drop dead gorgeous. Of course she does. Especially when I can't have her. Way to twist the knife.

When Ronnie shows up, he makes a beeline toward me. "Hey, man. You excited for the race?"

"A little nervous, but I usually am," I admit. I can't help it when my gaze slides over to where Jenni is talking to our moms. Both of the older women are dressed similarly to Jenni, with the hats and dresses.

I haven't built up the courage to talk to Jenni yet. There's this unspoken tension hanging between us. Not only are we broken up, but our horses are racing against each other, and we haven't trash-talked each other at all. It's a sad world when Jenni doesn't tease me about winning.

Ronnie pulls me aside. "I need to talk to you about something," he says, his voice low.

Hayden is sitting with the tablet I got him, lost in an educational video game about science that Maggie had recommended for him. I would have just let him play whatever, but Maggie insisted on the teacher-approved games she found from some website."

"What's up?"

"I had this long talk with Amanda last night, and I owe you an apology."

This ought to be good. That's the last thing I expected Ronnie to say. "Okay."

"She explained to me that she wasn't ever interested in me to begin with, and we kind of cleared the air. So this is me saying I'm sorry for misjudging you and saying for years that you betrayed me. If you hadn't gotten together with her, it wouldn't have made a difference. She wasn't going to date me either way."

"And what made you talk to her about this? Were you trying to ask her out now? You know that would be weird on so many levels, right?"

"Hey, don't judge me." Ronnie grins.

"So you're saying you wouldn't be mad at me if I wanted to date Jenni?"

"Nah, I already told her you two have my blessing."

"You did? And did she seem interested in dating me? Because that hasn't been the case in the past."

"I think you have a very good shot." He winks at me.

My stomach twists in knots, and my palms turn clammy. I wasn't expecting anything like this today. I've been trying so hard to get Jenni out of my mind and to stay focused on the race. I'd almost given up hope. But now it's surging through me, and all I can do is think about how badly I want to take her in my arms and hold her to me, stroke back her hair and tell her how very cherished she is.

The door opens, and Ashton comes in with Weston and his family.

"Look who's here!" Mom exclaims, rushing over to Ashton while Callie and Angel migrate to Jenni and Meera. "Come give your mama a hug."

He embraces her. "I've missed you, Mom."

"You're gone way too much. I know you came back to visit, but it's not enough. We miss you in Blue Mountain."

He pulls back from her. "I miss it here too."

"Have you met any new girls?" Mom asks.

"Mom, you know I don't have time for dating. We're going through a merger."

Typical Mom. Always the matchmaker.

"You've been off the hook for a while. It's your turn to have Mom pick out a girl for you," I say.

Dad speaks up. "I know just the girl for you, Ashton. Mr. Lee's daughter."

"That's not a bad idea," Mom says. "She's completely gorgeous and comes from a stellar family."

"That's new," Weston says. "Now Dad's getting involved in the matchmaking?"

"We're struggling with this merger. If Ashton were

to get in good with the owner's daughter, it could help us get through it," Dad says in a serious tone.

Ashton makes a face. "Chloe? I don't think so. She flat out hates me."

"I'm sure with a little bit of the old Keith charm, you can get her to warm up to you," Dad says with a grin.

Ashton groans.

I can't help but laugh. "It's for the good of the company."

~

*J*ust before the race begins, we all go outside so the horses can parade around for the people. Thunder is with his new jockey, Brian, and he's shown as his registered name of Ahead of the Storm, which is what the announcer will call him during the race. Next comes Valentine as Love Comes Quickly and his jockey, Christian.

"Go Thunder!" Hayden calls. "Boo Valentine!"

Jenni looks over at Hayden and laughs. "Valentine is going to win, you'll see, Hayden."

And for a minute, it feels like we're back to normal. And oh, how I long for that. Jenni snuggled up in my arms, teasing me about how her horse is going to win.

I want her back into my embrace more than anything. But there's no opportunity to talk to her.

Everything is craziness, and before I know it, we're heading to our front row seats, where we'll watch the race.

Jenni is sitting a ways down from me with her parents and Ronnie. I can't help but glance down at them every now and then to see how Jenni is doing. I feel like a kid in middle school, staring at his crush hopelessly from afar.

"Just go talk to her," Ashton says from beside me. "You're staring at her like a creeper."

"I am not. I'm staring at her like I'm desperate. Anyway, I can't talk to her right now. The race is about to begin."

"Excuses, excuses." He grins at me.

Just then the race begins, and horses burst from their stalls, bolting down the dirt track. Our racetrack is exactly one mile long, and there's only one lap from start to finish.

Thunder starts out in first place for the first half of the lap, but by the time they reach the opposite side of the track, Valentine pulls forward, taking the number one spot. Thunder's jockey urges him forward, but Valentine stays in the lead.

My fists clench, and I can hardly breathe. Not again. Even this new jockey isn't enough to beat Valentine. I've lost in love, and now I'm going to lose the race too.

But then Valentine goes down, and there's an

audible gasp that ripples through the audience.

It all happens so fast, but the horses don't stop. Seconds later, Thunder is across the finish line.

"And once again, Ahead of the Storm wins the Blue Mountain Derby!" the announcer calls. The crowd goes wild, and a vet rushes out to assist Valentine.

I've finally beaten Valentine, but the victory tastes sour in my mouth.

"Dad?" I look down to see Hayden's worried face. "Is Valentine going to be okay?"

I shake my head. "I don't know, buddy. The vet is down there right now, checking on him."

Jenni is crying, her hands covering her mouth. She cares so deeply for her horses. It always breaks her heart to see them struggling. And it breaks my heart to see her hurting. I want to go comfort her, but everyone around me is congratulating me.

Nothing about this feels right, and that's all I can think of as people are shaking my hand and hugging me, slapping me on the back.

I'm ushered to receive my prize, along with the trainer and the jockey. Music is playing and a garland of flowers is being placed around Thunder's neck.

Jenni is on the sidelines, taking all of it in while Valentine is with the vet.

I walk up to the stage where my trophy is waiting for me. The governor of Georgia is there, along with the mayor of Blue Mountain and many others I recognize as being big shots in town. Dad is up there with Mom and Jenni's parents as the owners of the Blue Mountain racetrack.

It's one of the biggest races of the year, right up there with the Kentucky Derby.

When I get up there, the governor smiles at me and hands me the trophy. When it's my turn to speak, I lean into the microphone, a camera focused on my face. "Ahead of the Storm and Brian raced beautifully today. Along with our fantastic trainer, they worked hard to earn this victory. But this win should have gone to Loves Comes Quickly. Had he not become injured, he would have won this race. So while I can't take away the win from Brian or my wonderful trainer, I will be taking my percentage of the purse money and will be giving it to Jenni Finley, the owner of Love Comes Quickly."

I turn and look at her. She's standing before me with shock on her face. "Jenni, I love you and I have for a long time. I know this win would have gone to you if it weren't for that injury."

"Would you look at that! True love is in the air," the announcer called. The crowd cheers, and Jenni looks up at me with tears streaming down her face.

When the ceremony is over, the crowd has dispersed, and the reporters have finished questioning me, I don't see Jenni anywhere. Eventually, I find her in the stables with Valentine.

"How's he doing?" I ask her.

She looks up to see me, eyes wide in surprise. "Oh, hi. I wasn't expecting to see you in here. I thought you'd be off celebrating."

"The celebration isn't as fun without you."

"Oh." She looks a bit unsure of what to say.

"So what did the vet tell you?"

"It's not good. They're saying he'll never race again. He's lucky he's still alive. Many horses don't recover from an injury like this."

I put a hand on her arm. "I'm sorry, Jenni. I know how much you love Valentine."

"Thank you for what you said up there, giving me the purse money like that. You didn't have to do that."

"I love you," I say.

She nods. "I know." She laughs a little. "You did mention that. In front of everyone."

My heart freezes for a moment. "Was that not okay?"

She smiles. "Langston, it was more than okay. I wasn't sure if you would still want me after you found out I couldn't have kids."

"Of course I want you. Being with you is the most important thing to me. Children can come in whatever way you want, whether that's adopting or fostering or just having Hayden. He's plenty."

"But you said you want a whole house full of kids." Her voice is small when she says it.

"That can be a house full of foster kids. Or kids we adopt. But the main part of this dream is to have you with me. I love you, Jenni Finely, and that will never change."

"You really mean that?"

"Of course I do."

"I love you too, Langston," she says.

"So what does that mean for us?" I ask.

She reaches out and takes my hand. "It means I want to be with you. If you'll have me."

I can't wait a moment longer. I pull her into my arms, and she melts into my embrace, feeling perfectly in place. "I'll have you. I want to keep you around forever."

"You sure about that? Forever is a really long time for you to put up with me."

I laugh. "I think I can handle it."

She steps on her tiptoes and covers my laugh with her mouth. Her sweet lips are on mine as I pull her tighter against my body. I deepen the kiss, and it stretches on until my head spins and I'm floating. I've never felt so much joy and bliss move through me in my life.

She pulls back and sighs against my lips, her breath tickling me, sending a shudder through me.

"You're really good at that. I think I might have to try it again sometime."

I can't keep the grin off my face. "I sure hope

you do."

~

*J*enni and I spend the rest of the weekend together. Our parents are overjoyed with the news that we're back together, and everyone is so kind and supportive toward Jenni now that her infertility secret is out.

Hayden seems to be the happiest of all, and when he found out Jenni was back in the picture, he gave her the biggest hug.

At the end of the weekend, I head out to take Hayden back to Amanda's place while Jenni soaks in a much needed bubble bath. Not that I was in there or anything. I just heard it was going to happen. Jenni's a wait-until-marriage kind of girl. And I'm okay with that, but it does get me thinking about marriage. I won't lie.

But regardless of that, I would be thinking of marriage. Because I love this woman so much, and it feels like this is a long time coming. I'm happy to date for a while longer, to make sure things are settling okay, but I'm already thinking about proposing within the next few months. Maybe my mom has rubbed off on me some. Or maybe I'm just a fool in love, but Jenni is wife material in every possible way.

Anyway, I don't want Jenni's parents getting any

more big ideas about that guy in India they think is so great for her. I'm happy to seal the deal before that guy can come near her.

"Dad, I had so much fun with you. It's not as fun at Mom's house. I love her and everything, but she's always so sick. She hardly pays attention to me anymore and I have to do a lot for myself because she's too tired to do it."

"It's okay for you to help her around the house a little, but if it's too much for you, I hope you know you can always tell me and I'll try to get your mom some help. Does she at least have a nurse who could come help her?"

He shakes his head. "No. She doesn't think she needs one."

I don't like the sound of that.

We pull up to her house, and Amanda comes out to the car, waving at Hayden. He climbs out and runs to hug her. "Hey, Hayden! Why don't you run inside and watch some TV? I need to talk to your dad for a minute."

"Okay, Mom." He looks back at me. "Bye, Dad. I love you."

My heart practically stops in my chest. He's never told me that before.

Amanda doesn't seem to miss it either. "Wow. He's come a long way," she says after he's in the house.

"He has. Things are going better than I'd expected

with him," I say.

"Hayden is like a different child these days. He's so happy to be here." She pauses for a minute and then raises her gaze to mine. "I owe you an apology, Langston. I never should have kept Hayden away from you like this. I've been in therapy since my diagnosis. I just found a new therapist here in town, and he's helped me see some of the reasons why I took off with Hayden back then. I was afraid you were going to turn out like my dad. He abandoned us when I was little. He had money too, but he found a new family and never paid us child support. So we really struggled growing up. When I discovered that I was pregnant, I just freaked out, thinking you would be just like my dad and leave us. So I left you first. But my therapist has helped me understand that I was dealing with trauma and likely have PTSD from my childhood abandonment. I see now that you're nothing like my dad. You're willing to be there for Hayden."

I nod. "All I want is whatever's best for Hayden."

"He's improved so much since you've been in his life."

"Does he know it wasn't my choice to stay away from him all those years?" I ask.

"He knows. But he doesn't understand everything about it. I just told him I'd explain it to him when he's older."

"What matters is that you're allowing him to be

with me now. We still have a lot of years together," I say. "But I do think he's going to need some help to get through all this so he's not stuck with childhood trauma that he has to sort through as an adult," I say. "How would you feel about starting family therapy?"

Amanda nods. "That would be wonderful."

"I'd be willing to pay for it, of course. And Amanda..."

"Yes?"

"If you need anything financially, medical bills, whatever, please let me know. Hayden is my son, and he lives half his life with you. I want him to be well provided for. So if you need help to come in and cook and help with Hayden, I'm more than happy to hire someone to provide that."

And here I was, just a few short weeks ago, accusing her of being a gold digger. But this is different. This time I'm happy to provide the assistance. She hasn't asked me for anything, and I realize now that I've misjudged her. If anything, she's the opposite of a gold digger.

"Thank you, Langston. I'll think about it, but I'll most likely be taking you up on that offer. Money is very tight for us."

The fact that she's saying that has shown that she's grown since she first came here. Maybe she's just realized that it's too hard to do it on her own. Or she's gotten a taste of what it's been like to have me help out with Hayden, and now she's realized that it's a relief to have help once in a while. "Money doesn't have to be tight for you. I owe you years of back child support. If I want my parental rights, I'm going to need to pay it to you."

Amanda gasps. "I never expected anything like that from you."

"I'm only doing what the court will dictate. This is coming straight from my lawyer. My paternity test came back positive, which we both knew would be the case."

Amanda nods. "I feel bad about arguing with you about Hayden going to public school. He's really struggling there. I'm happy to explore options about tutoring, if you're willing to let me be a part of the process."

"Of course. He's your son too."

Amanda looks like she's just had a weight taken off her shoulders. "Thank you. I'd better get back inside and check on Hayden."

"Sure." I wave goodbye and put the car into reverse as she heads back into the house. Peace washes over me as I realize how much anger and hurt I've been holding onto. I roll down the passenger side window, and she turns to face me. "Amanda? I need to tell you this. I forgive you. I want things to be good between us. That will be best for Hayden."

A grateful smile crosses her lips, and she raises a

hand to wave at me as I continue to back out of the driveway.

19

JENNI

The doorbell rings, and as I open it, the first thing I see is a blur of brown dashing into the house.

"Oh, you brought Sausage. I'm surprised he can run that fast with such a huge belly. You'd think he'd get rug burn from it dragging on the ground." I step on my tiptoes to kiss Langston.

"Mmm. I can get used to this."

"I hope you don't," I say.

"What?" Langston furrows his brow.

"I hope this always feels fresh and new. Just like it does today."

Langston smiles.

My heart flutters. "You don't know what your smile does to me, do you?"

That makes his grin grow even wider. "No, tell me all about it."

I trace a finger across his chest. "It makes me go weak at the knees, my breath catches in my throat, and my head starts to float."

"Your head floats?" Langston laughs. "Sounds like one of those campfire stories Hayden likes so much."

I smack his chest, which is so rock hard it hurts my hand. "Ow." I rub it. "You know what I mean."

"I do, actually. Because I feel the same way. Floating head and all," he says.

"This is why I adore you. Because you can joke around with me like this." I wrap my arms around his neck.

"That hasn't really changed." He loops his arms around my waist and kicks the front door shut.

"I'm glad. I think I've probably always loved you, although I may not have realized it. And it's the joking that does it for me."

He glances down over his shoulder. "It wasn't my hot tushie?"

I laugh. "That too. And your kind heart. Watching you with your boy really impacted the way I saw you. I mean, I always knew you were a great guy who was kind to others and took the time to say hello to your mom's knitting club friends, but when I saw you as a dad, even when it was unexpected and brand new, that's when I really started to fall harder and harder. Because I never expected to have a family, but when I saw you with yours, it was like this new possibility had opened for me. There was this boy who needed so much love, whose mom might not be around this time next year. I wanted to be there for him. And that never changed, even when we broke up. I knew I'd always be someone Hayden could rely on. He's stolen my heart."

"How could he not? He's the sweetest boy ever," Langston says.

A yowl sounds from the kitchen, followed by barking.

"Sounds like Sausage and Noodle have met," Langston says.

"That's right. You've never brought him over here before."

He shrugs. "There never really was a reason to."

"Then why bring him today?"

"Because today you and I are a couple. And there's nothing stopping us from having a future together. I figured this was the next step in our relationship. Letting our pets meet."

"Makes sense. But it doesn't seem to be going well." There's a loud crash coming from the kitchen. "We should probably go see what that noise is."

Langston and I rush into there to see the dinner I'd worked so hard on all over the floor with Sausage and Noodle both happily eating it. "Oh, no! I'd covered it and everything. Good thing I put it in a metal dish instead of glass."

"What is this?" Langston asks, gesturing to the dinner splattered all over my floor like some kind of modern art.

"Spaghetti sausage bolognese."

"Noodles and sausage? No wonder they like it so much."

I laugh. "You do have a good point. I should have known better than to make such a meal."

"Wait a second." Langston eyes me. "You made this?"

"Yes...?"

"Is it safe for the animals to eat?"

It takes me a minute to figure out what he means. And when I do, I scowl at him. "Very funny! I'm sure it's not that bad. I've been taking lessons with my chef."

"I heard about the cookies you made." Langston grimaces. "Word gets around, you know."

"We don't even know if this dinner is gross or not," I defend myself. "I've probably improved since then."

"You're welcome to scoop some off the floor and give it a try. You might have to fight the animals for it though."

"Ew." I walk over to the dish on the floor. "Look, there's a little still in here." I scoop a little out with a spoon and taste it. "Oh!" I run to the garbage and spit it out.

"You know Sausage probably had his head in that dish, right?"

I spit one more time. "I should have thought of that."

"It's okay, Sausage is pretty clean with his mouth."

"Yeah... I don't believe you. Anyway, they can have all they want. That stuff is disgusting. Maybe I'd better stick to picking out horses and leave the cooking for the chef."

"How's the horse shopping going, by the way?" Langston asks.

"Actually, pretty well. There's a new colt being born soon with an excellent pedigree. Both the dam and sire are from long lines of winning horses. Some have even won the Kentucky Derby."

"Sounds like Thunder is going to have some competition soon." Langston wiggles his brows at me.

"Oh, baby. I love it when you do that with your eyebrows."

He laughs and does it again, only more exaggerated this time, making him look ridiculous. But I love this adorable goofball.

I wrap my arms around him. "Should we order takeout?"

"Or we can even go somewhere," Langston suggests.

"Ooh. I like how you think. The diner?" I waggle my eyebrows at him.

He laughs. "Sure. I'll just have to drop Sausage at home. I don't think I want to leave him here unsupervised with Noodle. Those two make quite the destruction team."

"You know if we ever get married one day, we'll have to move them into the same house permanently, right?" I say.

"And Hayden too, don't forget."

"And whatever foster kids I get."

"Good grief, it'll be a zoo."

"We're going to have to buy a bigger house," I say, looking around. "I never really intended to raise kids here. It's too... white. Kids and white don't really go together well."

"You know I haven't proposed to you yet," Langston says.

"Oh, close enough. But we're being hypothetical anyway. It's good to talk about this stuff before we're in the middle of it. I'm a planner," I tell him.

"I like that about you. I tend to be more of a spontaneous kind of guy."

"And I like that about you," I say.

"We'll balance each other out, then." Langston pulls me toward him for another kiss.

And I gladly accept. I'm all about the smooching. And I don't care who it grosses out. I've never been so happy to be one of those annoying couples that have to kiss every five seconds.

~

"*I*'ll have the chicken sandwich," I tell Dolores when we're settled in our booth at Harvey's.

"And I'll have a bacon cheeseburger." Langston hands her the menu.

"That's what you always get," I say.

"I know what's good." He leans down and kisses my lips, and I savor every bit of the moment.

"Oh my goodness, look at how adorable the two of you are," Dolores says. "I always knew the two of you would be good together. Everyone in town could see the chemistry between you. You should have heard the knitting club going on about how Langston gave the purse money to his true love. They'll be talking about that for years. They say the footage of it went viral. You got any big plans of what to do with the cash?"

"Actually, I do," I say.

Langston turns to me. "Really? I hadn't heard this part."

"That's because I haven't told anyone yet."

"Well, let's hear it. You've got me curious now," Dolores says.

"I want to start a charity for foster children with it."

"Jenni, that's incredible," Langston says, his eyes tender.

"I've thought a lot about it."

"Have you heard any more about whether you can become a foster parent?" Langston asks.

"I'm still going through the process. It should take about six months before I'll be ready to have a kid."

"That's faster than getting pregnant and having one yourself," Dolores says. "Are you hoping to get a newborn or an older kid?"

"I'm open to either," I say. "I just want to help a kid out. In fact, I might even start an orphanage in India or someplace where kids are really in need."

"That's amazing, Jenni." Langston puts his hand over mine. "You really are an incredible woman."

"What about the charity?" Dolores asks. "What do you want to do with that?"

"I was thinking of doing two things. Maybe I can put together little care packages that helps a kid when they first get placed in a new home. That way, they will for sure have the basics. You know, like toiletries, a teddy bear, a comforting blanket. I'd have a clothing drive so there will be clothes provided for them. The foster parents get some money, but kids are still expensive, and there's no guarantee they're spending the money on the kids."

"That's a good point," Dolores says. "Not all the foster parents out there are as kind and selfless as you, Jenni. Whoever you get will be very lucky to have you."

"Thank you, Dolores," I say, sipping the soda she'd brought earlier. "One other thing I want to do is to provide help for the kids after they get out of foster care so they can get the training they need to be able to have a decent career."

"You're full of ideas," Langston says.

"I've been thinking about this a long time. The more I research the topic, the more excited I get."

"Best of luck to you," Dolores says. "Now I'd better get back to the kitchen with your order before Mr. Harvey notices that I'm over here talking my head off."

After she leaves, I turn to Langston. "I love her. I could talk to Dolores all day."

"Maybe we can have her over to a barbecue sometime."

"I'd really like that. And then we can be the ones bringing her burgers. Let her put her feet up for once." I lean in to kiss Langston. "Another reason why I love you so much."

"I still haven't told you about the conversation I had with Amanda," Langston says.

"You talked to her again since she apologized?"

"Yeah, last night. She told me that she's been struggling with mental illness her entire life. I hadn't really realized that, but apparently, it runs in her family."

"That would explain some of her erratic behavior," I say. "And the fact that her family is all estranged. Mental illness can do that to families."

"Think of how she disappeared from our marriage without an explanation and never telling me about

Hayden. She struggled with paranoia, and that's why she left in the first place. She was convinced that I was going to abandon her with the baby like her dad did to her when she was little."

"That's so sad, Langston. It was really big of her to tell you that. It must have taken a lot of courage on her part, to be so honest."

"I've seen a lot of growth in Amanda. I just hope that she's able to get the best care possible. I don't want to see Hayden going through the loss of a mother."

"I heard that you were offering her money."

"Yes, all the back child support as well as the alimony she deserves. She was too proud to ask for it before, but she can get better treatment if she has the opportunity. There are some procedures that can be pretty pricey and aren't covered by insurance. She has a better shot of beating her cancer if she can afford the care."

"Langston, that's incredible. So you think Amanda has a chance to go into remission?"

He shrugs. "I don't know. But she's the mother of my son, and I'll do all I can to save him from the pain of losing a mother."

"That only makes me love you that much more."

He lowers his head to mine, our noses touching. "I love you too," he whispers.

"Look at the two of you being all mushy."

I look up to see Brensen and Ronnie coming

toward us and realize Brensen is the one who'd just spoken.

"Hey, guys." Langston waves.

"What's up, man?" Ronnie asks.

"When did you get into town, Brensen?" I ask. He's been over in Africa on a spiritual journey, trying to find himself.

"Just today. Stopped by for a bite to eat and ran into Ronnie on my way into the building. I wasn't expecting to see you two here either. I heard you were together, and I had to come home to see it for myself."

"Come sit down with us, guys," I invite.

"You sure we won't be interrupting?" Brensen asks.

"Not at all. But I can't promise there won't be a little PDA on our part." I laugh.

"I might lose my appetite," Ronnie jokes, climbing into the booth across from where Langston and I are cuddled up. Brensen slides in next to him.

"It can't be worse than when you took Felicia out on a date, Ronnie. You guys were sucking face the entire time." Langston has a grossed-out expression as he says it.

"Who's Felicia?" Brensen asks.

"Some girl from college Ronnie had the hots for," Langston explains. "Whatever happened to her anyway?"

Ronnie shrugs. "She ended up getting married and having a ton of kids."

"Forever the bachelor," Brensen says. "Join the club."

"What about you, Brensen?" I sip my soda. "Any girls on the horizon?"

"Possibly."

"You're always so mysterious about women," Ronnie says.

Brensen grins. "I don't like to kiss and tell."

"But it's so much more fun when you do." It's true too. I'm all about hearing about other people's love lives.

"Which never happens," Langston says. "That makes me think he's hiding something."

Brensen only smiles bigger. "Oh, man. This is fun. It's been ages since we just sat here at Harvey's shooting the breeze."

Dolores shows up with our food and takes Ronnie and Brensen's orders.

I dig into my chicken sandwich while Brensen tells us all about Kenya. "I want to start a nonprofit over there to help all the poverty-stricken children there."

"Hey, me too," I pipe up. "I was just saying I want to start an orphanage in India. Maybe we could have one in Kenya too."

"I know some people who could help make that happen," Brensen says. "But it looks like Dad wants me to come back here and work for the company."

"Is that the real reason you're back?" Langston asks.

"Yep. But I did want to see you two love birds too. Even if you are completely nauseating."

"So it's not just me then?" Ronnie throws his hands up in the air.

Dolores comes back with drinks and refills, and Brensen and I start brainstorming how the nonprofit might work. "I've worked with several nonprofits while I've been over there. Dad is cutting off my trust money unless I agree to work for the company. So I ran out of options. If I want to make a difference, I'm going to need access to my money."

"It's always been a requirement that we work for him to get the entirety of our trust money. Having the family running this business is very important to him," Langston explains.

"So does this mean you're back for good?" I ask.

"I'll still be able to travel to Kenya to check on things, but yes. I've moved back, and I'm currently living with Mom and Dad until I can get my own place in town. Which should be soon. Mom is already pressuring me to ask a few of her friends' daughters out, and I need a bit of my own space.

Langston laughs. "There is definitely is a plus side to having a girlfriend. You get Mom off your back."

"Not really. She's going to pressure you about when you plan to pop the question now."

Langston grins. "I'm fully aware of it. Mom and I have already had that conversation. I've learned that if you keep her in the loop, she gets off your back pretty quickly. She just wants to see that progress is being made."

"You make her sound like quite the taskmaster," I tease.

"You have no idea," Langston drawls.

Ronnie quirks a brow. "I'm pretty sure she does."

"That's a good point. Jenni has been around for everything." He catches my gaze and reaches under the table to take my hand. "And she's not going anywhere if I have anything to say about it."

"You couldn't get rid of me if you tried," I say.

"Well, I'll never try, so this is a pointless conversation."

"They really are nauseating," Brensen tells Ronnie.

"Sounds like you're next." Ronnie eyes Brensen. "Unless you have a woman you've been keeping a secret."

Brensen shakes his head. "It's nothing like that. She's just a friend."

"Ohhh. So there is someone," Langston exclaims. "I knew it! You're way too much of a stud to not have a girl after you."

"That's the thing. She's not after me at all. We're just friends," Brensen tells us.

"Ouch. Friend zoned!" Ronnie crows. "Sounds like what Amanda did to me."

"Oh yeah, you were into Amanda," Brensen says.

"Wouldn't it be weird if you ended up with her and then became Hayden's stepdad?"

"Yeah, I realize that now. But Amanda isn't interested anyway. She never was."

"Weren't you and Langston fighting over her for years?" Brensen wants to know.

"That's all resolved now," Langston explains. "No need to bring it up again."

"It sounds like you two have done some growing up since I talked to you last."

Langston laughs. "That's an understatement. For me, at least. I've had to take a crash course on parenting. And not just any kid either. One that has a multitude of issues to sort out."

"But it's nothing that you can't work through," I say, taking his arm and wrapping my arm around it. "You just have to take it one day at a time. You'll get there."

Langston looks down into my eyes. "Thank you, babe. That means a lot."

Ronnie grins. "Oh, it's babe now?" He's come a long way since we first started fake dating. What a relief.

"It might as well be," Langston tells me in a husky voice that I'm sure Ronnie doesn't want to hear.

"I like it." It fits. I've always wanted to have a guy call me a pet name like that. And what better person than Langston?

Who says dreams don't come true? If it hadn't been for my infertility, I never would have thought to look into foster care or to start orphanages in both India and Kenya. Look at all the amazing things that are coming from the fact that I can't bear a child of my own.

This is a dream come true, but it's a dream I hadn't realized I'd had until recently. It's funny how life works out.

I lean into the amazing man next to me, my heart fuller than it's ever been.

So this is what a happily ever after feels like.

EPILOGUE

Brensen

*S*ix months later

Langston's house is packed when I get there for his engagement party. Everyone is out in the backyard surrounding the grill, sitting out at tables spread across the lawn beneath maple trees that are bright orange and red. It's still not that cold outside, but this is Georgia, after all. It never gets much of a winter to begin with. It's more like fall slowly turns into spring with a few chilly days in between.

Still, it's been a while since I've seen the seasons changing. Kenya doesn't get much of a fall.

Powell is manning the grill, stacking up piles of chicken legs, hamburgers, hot dogs, brats, and steaks. There's a table laden with food, including potato salad, coleslaw, green salad, baked beans, and a variety of desserts. Knowing Powell's cooking, it's probably all delicious too.

"You sure know how to throw a shindig," I tell Langston when I come up to him where he's standing by his new fiancée. She's holding a bundle in her arms. "Is this the new little one?" I peek into the blue blanket to see a sweet newborn's face.

"Yes, he just arrived last week. This is James, our new foster baby."

"Nice to meet you, little fella," I coo down to the tiny person.

He yawns, and his tiny eyes flutter open. He begins squirming in Jenni's arms, opening his mouth and twisting his head from side to side.

"Looks like he's hungry," Mom says.

Mom's ability to figure out what a baby wants baffles me. "How can you tell? The little stinker isn't even crying."

"Grandmothers just know these things." Mom grins. "Give him to me, Jenni. I'll make sure he gets a bottle."

"What's the story with this one?" I ask after she's left.

"He was left at the Blue Mountain fire station. Poor little guy." Jenni looks over to where Mom took him. "Can you imagine just being abandoned like that?"

"It's a good thing he won't remember any of this.

He'll just grow up to know that he has amazing foster parents who love him very much." I have to say, I really admire Jenni that she wants to help these kids in need.

"And wonderful grandparents." He gazes over to where Mom is speaking baby talk to him and coaxing him to take a bottle.

"Are you thinking of adopting him?" I ask.

Jenni nods. "That's the plan. We weren't sure we'd be able to get a newborn, but since this baby came from Blue Mountain, they gave him to me. I'm sure it helped that the workers and I get along really well. Especially since they found out I'm starting a nonprofit to help foster kids. I'll be starting in this area, too."

"Are you hoping to take it bigger?"

She nods. "Eventually."

"That's incredible." I clap my hands together. "Is the plan to move into Langston's place after you're married?"

"Yes. Eventually, we'd like to build an addition to the house."

"Really?" I ask. "It's not a bad idea."

"Yeah," Langston explains, "At first, we talked about getting an entirely new house built, but Jenni likes how my land connects with her parents' land. So we decided to make it work here."

"We won't need to do any additions for a while still." Jenni looks up at the home. "For now, our main focus is getting the wedding planned."

"And we don't have long to plan it either," Langston adds.

"Oh, you've set a date already?" I ask.

Jenni nods. "We're hoping for a Christmas wedding."

"That's only couple months." Way to rush things.

"I know. Mom is scrambling." Langston nods. "We just don't see a reason to wait. Jenni has a nanny for James, but it's still a lot on her. It'll be easier if we're married to help each other out with the kids."

"Well, good for you," I say. "I'm really happy for the both of you." And I mean it. It's nice to see Langston finding his true love.

"Who knows?" Jenni teases. "Maybe you're next."

I laugh. "I think I'm going to grab a plate of food."

"Help yourself," Langston offers. "There's plenty."

Dad catches up to me when I'm loading my plate with a ribeye and a skewer of grilled veggies. "How's the Williams acquisition coming along?"

"I'm struggling to get along with some of the other members in the office, to be honest. I think they resent the fact that I've just been in Africa for so many years and not working my way to the top like they have been."

"You're my son. You own a percentage of this company. That's just how life works."

But it's not going to fix the fact that I'm the most hated guy in the office. No one likes an entitled guy. It means I'm going to have to work much harder than the rest of them to convince them I've earned my place. I may have shown up unexpectedly at the top, but that doesn't mean I'm going to shove it in their faces either. All I can do is keep my head down and work hard.

My phone buzzes in my pocket, and I pull it out to see a text.

Faith: *I was able to get my Visa. I'm coming to the US. I should be there within a month.*

Me: *That's incredible. But I was hoping to have your help in Kenya with my nonprofit.*

Faith: *I guess I'll have to help you in Georgia then.*

Me: *Georgia? I thought you were moving to Washington D.C.*

Faith: *Last minute change. We'll be in Atlanta now.*

Me: *I guess I'll see you around then.*

When she doesn't respond, I slip my phone back into my pocket. My headquarters for the beginnings of the nonprofit I'm starting is in Atlanta. It will be perfect to have Faith there. Maybe she can help out. I've really missed having her around.

After I left Kenya, she became a nanny to a US Ambassador, who ended up going home. I'd thought I'd have to go back to Kenya to see Faith.

After moving back to Georgia, I got my own place in Blue Mountain, but then I ended up spending most of my time in Atlanta at the company so I bought a condo in a high rise, the same building where Weston and Callie have a place for when he has to work at the main office.

I hate working at the Keith Enterprise headquarters and would prefer to work from Blue Mountain. But for now, that doesn't seem to be possible.

I take a seat at a table, and Jenni and Langston sit with me.

Jenni leans across the table in a conspiratorial way. "We want to know who you were texting just now."

"What makes you think I was texting someone important?"

"By the look on your face. It was clearly someone you like."

"Is it the girl who friend zoned you?" Langston asks.

I sigh. "There really is no privacy in this family, is there?"

Jenni grins. "Nope."

"You fit right in. You're going to be as bad as Callie and Mom. Ariana too. They've all been hounding me to start dating since I've been home."

"What's holding you back?" Langston asks. "Your *friend*?"

"Something like that." But the truth is, it's exactly that. Faith has never seen me as anything more than just a best friend. And she's all I can think about.

But I'm not in the mood to go deeper in the subject, or next thing I know, they'll be pressuring me to tell her how I really feel and blah, blah, blah. And if I were to reveal my feelings to Faith, I could lose her friendship. I'm just getting her back. The last thing I want to do is mess everything up. She's the main reason I didn't want to leave Kenya. She's amazing. Like the sun. Always bright, hardworking, and optimistic. Never speaking a word against anyone.

"How's the racing going, guys? I'm sorry I missed the race last week. I was working late at the office."

"Jenni's new horse, Blazing Star, is taking out all the competition. Including me," he groans.

I laugh. "That sounds about right."

"It's the story of my life."

"Maybe it's time to retire Thunder and move onto a younger horse," I suggest.

"As much as I hate to admit that, you might be right. Thunder didn't even place in the last race he did."

"I might try getting a horse myself." I gaze out to the pasture where the horses are chowing down. "All this racing stuff looks like a lot of fun."

"You should try it," Jenni says. "There's nothing like the rush of seeing your horse cross that finish line before all the others."

"I have a feeling with you around, I'll never experience that." I laugh.

"Probably not," Langston says. "I can't win now that Blazing Star is in the picture. But it doesn't matter." He kisses Jenni's cheek. "I've already won the woman of my dreams."

I glance over to see Hayden holding James with Amanda's assistance. "And your long-lost son."

"I'm the luckiest guy alive. But that doesn't mean we haven't had our rough patches."

"It's interesting that you invited Amanda to your engagement party." I look out to see her smiling down at James and talking baby talk to him.

"We've made our peace with her." Langston glances over in their direction too.

"She looks like she's feeling better." I've been out of the loop with her progress since I've been working so hard at the company. "I take it her treatments have been working?"

"Like you wouldn't believe. She just found out last week that her cancer's in remission."

"You're kidding," I exclaim. "That's fantastic news."

"It really is." Jenni nods. "She's going to move into my old house with Hayden after Langston and I marry. I offered to rent it to her. Now that the court papers are signed, and she's getting the proper amount of child support as well as her back pay, she can afford my place, and we wanted Hayden to have a nicer place to live. The neighborhood where they were before was a little rough."

"I want a safe environment for my son," Langston says.

"How's the family therapy going?" I ask.

"Remarkably well," Jenni replies. "Hayden was having nightmares when Langston and I first got together, but with therapy, he's been able to talk through his feelings some."

"Amanda too," Langston adds. "Every other week, we have her join us. It's been a really great experience."

"Now we just need to figure out how to be good parents to a newborn."

"That's a new experience for both of us," Langston says. "I can't believe Amanda did all of this alone when she had Hayden. We have both of us, my mom, and a nanny, and we're still exhausted."

"Don't forget my mom too," Jenni says.

"Yes, your mom has been wonderful," Langston agrees.

"But Amanda has you now." I look back over to where she's taking the baby from her kid. "And she's lucky to have you both. You've been great to Hayden. And to her."

"We do our best," Langston says.

They really do seem to have everything figured out.

I watch them with longing. They have such a beautiful family. I'm not sure it's in my future to have one myself.

Maybe I'll be the forever bachelor of the family. It certainly won't be Ashton.

Will it be enough to love Faith from afar, always stuck in the friend zone?

It will have to be. Because it's all I have, and that's at least better than nothing.

But there's something heartbreaking about accepting that fact.

~

Do you want to find out if Brensen ever gets his happily-ever-after?

Read Flirting With My Billionaire Bestie, coming soon.

ABOUT THE AUTHOR

Cindy Ray Hale loves to write romcoms set in small towns and has been writing and publishing books since 2012, all the while, laughing at her own funny stories. She is married to the sweetest guy and has a blended family with him, consisting of seven kids.

She loves nerding out on video games, creating book covers, and drinking too much caffeine. When she can find a moment, she loves to sing and play the piano and often includes acting and singing somewhere in her stories.

She was born and raised in the hills of Tennessee in a large crazy family and as an adult, has moved all over the United States. She's finally settled down in a small town in the mountains of western Virginia where she loves to go hiking, boating, and dig in her garden.

Want to be the first to know about a sale or a new release for Cindy's books? Visit www.cindyrayhale.com to sign up for her newsletter and get a free book.

Are you a superfan or a book reviewer? Join Cindy's Facebook group Cindy Ray Hale's Superfans to be the first to hear about new releases and the chance to get your hands on an Advanced Reader Copy of one of her upcoming novels.

Subscribe to her YouTube Channel to listen to her books free! @CindyRayHale

facebook.com/cindyrayhaleauthor
twitter.com/cindyrayhale
instagram.com/cindyrayhale
bookbub.com/profile/cindy-ray-hale
amazon.com/stores/Cindy-Ray-Hale/author/B00GEMM4IO